TAKING THE WALL

TAKING THE WALL

JONIS *A*GEE

—— *stories* ——

COFFEE HOUSE PRESS

COPYRIGHT © 1999 by Jonis Agee
COVER + BOOK DESIGN by Kelly Kofron
COVER PHOTOGRAPH by David Harvey/NGS Images
AUTHOR PHOTOGRAPH by Richard Gray

Some of these stories have been previously published in the following: *Michigan Quarterly Review, Lynx, Prairie Schooner, Nebraska Review.*

Coffee House Press is an independent nonprofit literary publisher supported in part by a grant provided by the Minnesota State Arts Board, through an appropriation by the Minnesota State Legislature, and in part by a grant from the National Endowment for the Arts. Significant support has also been provided by The McKnight Foundation; Lannan Foundation; Jerome Foundation; Target Stores, Dayton's, and Mervyn's by the Dayton Hudson Foundation; the Bush Foundation; General Mills Foundation; The Lila Wallace Reader's Digest Fund; St. Paul Companies; Butler Family Foundation; Honeywell Foundation; Star Tribune Foundation; James R. Thorpe Foundation; the law firm of Schwegman, Lundberg, Woessner & Kluth, P.A.; and many individual donors. To you and our many readers across the country, we send our thanks for your continuing support.

Coffee House Press books are available to the trade through our primary distributor, Consortium Book Sales & Distribution, 1045 Westgate Drive, Saint Paul, MN 55114. For personal orders, catalogs, or other information, write to: Coffee House Press, 27 North Fourth Street, Suite 400, Minneapolis, MN 55401.

Good books are brewing at coffeehousepress.org.

LIBRARY OF CONGRESS CIP INFORMATION
Agee, Jonis
    Taking the wall : stories / by Jonis Agee
      p.   cm.
    ISBN 1-56689-088-8 (alk. paper)
    1. United States—Social life and customs—20th century Fiction.
  2. Automobile racing drivers—Family relationships Fiction.
  3. Automobile racing drivers—United States Fiction
  4. Automobile racing—United States Fiction. I. Title.
  PS3551-G4T35 1999
  813'.54—dc21
                                 99-35463
                                    CIP

10 9 8 7 6 5 4 3 2 1

Printed in Canada

for Talbot Guy

Thanks to Dale Jarrett, Mark Martin, Dale Earnhardt, Jeff Gordon, Bill Elliot, Dick Trickle, Terry and Bobby LaBonte, Ricky Rudd, Chad Little, and all the other wonderful drivers who make my weekends an adventure. Special thanks to Lon Otto who continues to be the finest friend and critic any writer could have despite his lack of interest in creatures with four wheels. And thanks to Sharon Oard Warner whose drawl and wit help keep me off the wall. Thanks to Kelly Allen who has helped in a hundred ways to make life simple enough to have time and energy to write. And always love to my daughter Brenda who brings such humor and light to my life.

contents

A circle, a circumference, an endless line,
the wheel is our motion, our fortune, our fate:
a damned fast car.

Good to Go

Well, we'd mortgaged everything but the baby, and Donnie tore the rear spoiler half off, lost his downforce, and that was about it. Track came up and smacked him silly. That was the last time we had any money to speak of. Since then it's been working at Wal-Mart and a '78 Olds with a hole in the floor big enough for J.P. to lose a sneaker through. Last time it rained I was ankle deep in water floating down the blacktop to Cedar Rapids. Donnie's too busy welding other people's cars back together to put that piece permanent over the floor. He's the nice guy the neighbors call at suppertime to come fix their mower or disposal. We're making love and somebody needs a spark plug. Same thing when he was racing. Bob there needed to finish high enough to keep his sponsor. Frankie Jr. had the wife's medical bills, and then there was the night Spanus came to look over Owen Brach for the Craftsman Truck Series. Donnie, I said, Donnie we got bills and babies too.

You pay for your mistakes in racing, my stepdad Walter says. You miss the setup and you take the wall. Walter has his own garage and Donnie was working there when we met. It's funny, that's where Mom met Walter too. She'd driven me and a car full of stuff through one whole night to get away from her boyfriend and Versailles, Missouri. Needed gas and an answer for the terrible thumping in the rear end. Walter's Friendly Service squatted on the outskirts of town in possession of twenty acres of abandoned cars and a fairly new, pink and white doublewide mobile home that sat in its own pavilion surrounded by a fence of half-buried tractor trailer tires painted white. Mom always loved their half-moon scallops, and admired a man who would take the time, she said. She's gone, of course. Hers was a restless heart, and even Walter understands how she came to leave with the UPS man right after Donnie showed up. She'd been going away for a while, her eyes shiny with longing of an impossible kind whenever she watched those long legged country singers on CMT. Dwight Yoakam, Alan Jackson, you know the ones. She loved us, Walter and me, with as much as was free inside her, but the rest of her, well, it was always going someplace else, and she was just the wagging tail to its dog.

The UPS man was half-Indian too. That's what she told me the night she left. Walter and Donnie were at the fairgrounds, watching the Demolition Derby that was our town's annual contribution to the Fourth of July. The fireworks would follow and I was getting ready to go out and climb on the roof of the garage to watch. It was my general policy to avoid men wrecking cars on purpose whenever possible. You see, I had that whole twenty acres of torn sheet metal and smashed windows to grow up in. It didn't take a genius to figure out the evolution. That particular family tree don't branch, I'd tell Donnie later.

Mom always seemed to leave places at night. She wasn't a Monday morning, new start kind of person. She waited and waited for her time, and it always came somewhere between eight and ten at night. She'd make all her decisions then, like one of those nocturnal animals whose brain clicked awake as soon as the sun set. I used to wonder what kept her with us as long as she did stay. I helped her pack that night. Maybe that was wrong of me, but I personally wrapped the pressed-glass swan vase she got from her Ozarks grandmother. I was afraid she'd be in such a hurry she'd forget it or not take enough care packing it, and I couldn't bear the picture of her standing there later with the pieces in her hands, knowing she'd lost something precious forever, something she could never ever make up or come back to. She was that kind of person. You wished her well. She had enough desire and longing for all of us, and I was just glad it was her having to drive away from places in the middle of the night, not me. My desire does not have geographical dimensions, I tell Donnie when he suggests we move to the other side of town.

I miss her. Miss how she could make Walter smile and shake his head and turn fast as a pony on a dime and try to chase her down when she teased him in the middle of work. She never minded the grease prints on her blouse and white-blonde hair or the burn his red stubble made around her mouth when they got to the house. Walter's not too sad now, you understand, he's just lost a little bit of air. He's skinnier somehow, like Mom took the fat out of his life. Now he has to live on lean and while that's good in some ways, it's really less than before and neither of us can forget that. I know he wishes I was more like her, that I'd treat Donnie the same way so he could get that lift out of watching us. But like I said, I'm not that kind of person. I leave Donnie to his work, and he leaves me to mine. Mine being J.P., working part-time at Wal-Mart, and keeping track of the salvage business.

It's funny how those twenty acres of cars became my responsibility. As a kid I wanted a horse, begged and pleaded, tried to win one in contests, prayed for some old man to leave me his money anonymously. I knew no woman would do anything that foolish, but I still believed in the crazy goodness of men then. One night at supper Walter put his fork down, finished chewing his Salisbury steak, swallowed, and announced that he too had been thinking hard about my problem, and he thought he'd found a solution. I could have a horse as soon as I cleared enough of those cars away for a pasture. He figured ten acres would be a good start. It was the kind of announcement filled a kid with despair and hope both, tangled impossibly, leaving you sleepless with frantic planning. I was twelve so it still seemed fairly simple to sell or move enough cars for my horse. First, I decided, I'd have to catalog the cars and make a list I could send around. Someone would want those good parts. Later when I came up with the plan to have them hauled away to a place that crushed and recycled metal, Mom gave a gentle shake of her head. Honey, she said, Walter loves those cars, no matter what he said.

And so it was that I came to see that I would have to defeat Walter's love for one of my own, and the unfairness of it struck me for the first time as what it meant to be helpless in the face of your own desire. It had been a year since our bargain, and while I had increased the salvage business by a good amount with my little catalog, the cars never seemed to do more than grow more hollow, piece by piece, until their skeletons rested mossy and black among the weeds that grew higher and higher, and as much as anything they came to resemble untended graves.

What I had ignored was the fact that new cars would be added as out in the world they grew old and died, got wrecked or totaled, and people in them escaped or died. It came to me after a while to look suspiciously at some cars: the black Trans Am that took Buddy Holden's legs, the green and white Chevy pickup that developed a fatal attraction for the Burlington Northern train taking the whole Smithen family with it. By the time I was fourteen, I began to dread spring nights when the high school seniors would scatter their lives like dandelion seeds to the wind in cars that the next day would be hauled through our gates and deposited, sometimes with blood stains still visible on the upholstery and the jagged glass of the windshield.

I avoided those cars on my walks then, hated to see the cats tip-toeing across the hoods, leaving dusty little prints, then pausing at the smashed windshield, sniffing the air, and pumping their tails slowly up and down before springing inside. Mice and field rats seemed to like those cars best. It took me a while to get on any sort of basis with those cars. Sometimes it never happened. I'd try to sell their parts fast, cheap, get their lethal hearts out of there. Still do.

There is one car I don't ever advertise though. One I'd never sell a piece of. I'd as soon bury it, but for Walter. Kids come around wanting a rocker panel, a header, a camshaft. I tell them take anything but leave that one up by the fence alone. I keep it close, you see.

Donnie and I might never have gotten together if it hadn't been for Mom's car, the one that drove us into Walter's heart. It was an old Chevy Malibu with the paint worn off to gray and rust eating its way up the doors and down through the roof and hood. The trunk lock was gone from the time we'd lost the key, and the lid was held down by a bungee cord. Walter always threatened to do something about that car, but the best thing he could manage was to keep the engine strong after he'd dropped in a new one when it became clear that we were staying on more or less permanently in the doublewide. The motor came from an old Buick Roadmaster and was really too big for the Malibu, which made it a spicy little car that spun its wheels at every stop sign and lifted its front end if you stepped on the gas too hard. When the muffler got a hole, it sounded like the hottest car in town. Walter didn't believe in new cars, and Mom didn't care. I was the only one interested in something with shine and glitter, I guess, since I'd had to give up on the horse. I needed to satisfy myself somehow, and I still thought it was going to be something with four legs or four wheels. I had no idea it was going to be Donnie until he came to lean over the engine one day while I was checking the oil. He took the dipstick out of my hand and wiped it clean between two fingers he rubbed off on his jeans while he stuck the stick back in and pulled it out again. Squinting in the sunlight at the light new oil, he nodded as if we'd come to some essential agreement and put it back in the hole. I was watching his tan arm with the veins popping and the hair bleached blonde, the thick wrist with that bone sticking up and it made my stomach hollow with want.

You keep your engine tight, he said lifting the air filter off and checking the white folds for dirt. Big mother, isn't it? He screwed the wingnut down and jiggled the hoses, running his hands down their lengths for tears. Think I could drive her sometime?

He pressed the fan belt for give and nodded with satisfaction. Turn it on, he instructed.

We won money almost from the start, drag racing Mom's car on the blacktop three miles away in the middle of the night. Donnie put on a glass pack muffler, leg pipes, and dual exhausts, then went to work on the engine. Walter watched us out of the corner of his eye, kept Donnie working late as possible, and Mom fell in love with the UPS man.

The first time we did it wasn't in the backseat of the car though. It was in the middle of Heison's oatfield. We'd won a hundred and fifty dollars that night from some guys from Iowa City, and they'd gotten so pissed we'd had to take off and hide. Wasn't hard since we knew every farm and field road in the county, and we'd been necking on most of them. That night the wind was blowing hot with an edge of cool rain we could smell from someplace not too far away, so we flung open the car doors and ran into the middle of the field and lay down making angels in poor Heison's oats. In the morning, he'd think it was deer and threaten to go hunting out of season, but we didn't care. The grain was coming ripe and it smelled nutty and sweet as the wind pushed it around and about us like big heavy waves of hissing water. Donnie undid the only button fastening his shirt, and when I saw that smooth tan chest and stomach, I knew what I was going to do. I sat up and pulled my T-shirt over my head. He shrugged out of his shirt, and the wind moaned in the trees on either side of the field, tossing the sound back and forth over our heads as he lay down on top of me, and I licked the salt sweet sweat on his cheek as sandpapery as a cat's tongue. Then I let him put his thick oil-dark fingers everywhere he wanted.

Afterwards we lay there side by side while the storm came up and lightning struck the cornfield on the other side of the trees, and we could feel the razor jolt ripping along the ground in all directions. We made love again in the muddy oats, naked, our clothes drowned somewhere beside us. At dawn we drove home, and Walter and Mom met us at the door. Donnie moved in that day. It only took ten days to get us married. I was sixteen. Donnie was nineteen. But that isn't the car I'm talking about.

I don't know how we moved from drag racing to oval tracks. Probably the junked racer we got the year J.P. was born. I'd just turned eighteen and was still running the salvage. Donnie and I had our own trailer now. Not a doublewide, but it was enough. We had the twenty acres, the garage, and the office to run around in, and Mom and I spent time together too, so I never felt confined or anything. Some days, I admit, while I was nursing J.P., I'd sit at the kitchen window and look out across my cars and think of them as horses, grazing in the snow there, pawing to get down to last summer's grass, their coats shaggy as sheepdogs. I had bays and blacks mostly, with one or two chestnuts or grays. But mostly I liked the good reliable colors, nothing too fancy, nothing that showed dirt or too much personality. I'd read that the browns were best, that all other horses wanted to be brown, that's why the palominos and whites kept rolling in the dirt. It could be true, I decided, leaning into the tugging weight of J.P. at my nipple. It would be nice to go out there and call and have your horses come galloping up to the fence for a carrot. To be able to pat their warm chests, to bury your face in their thick necks, to feel their hot breath blowing on the back of your head. The cars looked forlorn out there in the winter, the only tracks from the dogs trotting up and down the rows, inspecting the ranks like visiting generals. The deer don't bother coming in the salvage yard. People work less on their cars that time of year too, so it could be peaceful and lonely out there, especially when I was nursing. That winter Mom got a job in town at the drugstore, so she wasn't around much either. That way she could see the UPS man more often, I guess, though I didn't know it at the time.

The racecar showed up on the back of a flatbed from Mason City. "Lady says to tell you she doesn't want to see this thing again," the driver announced and backed the rig through the gates. I had him put it right up front so I could go over it when I had time without having to wade through the deep snow. Donnie could use the tractor to drag it back down with the others later. But that's not what happened. I fell asleep after J.P. was done nursing, and by the time I woke up and got us both bundled for the outdoors, it was well past lunch and Donnie was back from his morning job driving school bus for the kindergartners. He'd found the number two red and black Pontiac and was already inside trying to fix the ignition box. Thank you, oh thank you, thank you, he crawled out the window and kissed me and J.P. enough that I couldn't tell him the truth. And so Donnie came to believe that I'd given him the Christmas present he'd always wanted, and I came to be the biggest liar in the family. At least I was then.

So we went racing, taking Walter with us too when he could find someone to work weekends at the station. Mom was working long hours in town, or so we thought, and we were too busy to notice all the changes that were taking place. Me, I thought it was Dwight Yoakam she was in love with, and what was the harm of that, I'd ask Donnie late at night at the track, snuggling in our truck bed camper, J.P. in his own little bed on top of the flip-down table we ate at.

Once in a while we'd win, but it wasn't anything like the drag racing we'd done. We were broke all the time, borrowing from Mom and Walter, taking extra jobs, the both of us, finding J.P.'s clothes and toys in the secondhand stores, rummage and yard sales. Donnie had that true believer look in his eyes though, and I don't think he noticed how it was going for the baby and me. I'd spend my time trying to rustle up deals on parts off flyers I'd make during the week at home, and trying to line up what Donnie needed for his car too. I took to keeping J.P. on a piece of clothesline tied around his waist and mine. Got dirty looks for that, and some laughs, but it was safety really. We were both about half deaf from the roaring engines. But I remembered what it was like all those years before when I'd wanted a horse more than anything else in the world and how it had seemed like both the easiest and the hardest, most distant thing that could happen, and I could not deny Donnie that one little corner of his dream.

Then we went through a time when everything seemed to click. Walter was helping with the engine and Donnie was driving like Richard Petty. Our life started moving faster, we bought a newer pickup and then a decent used car for me. We went to bigger tracks and got to know some of the other drivers and their families. The crowds started cheering for us once in a while. That lasted a year and a half, with our dreams tumbling out hot and fresh like clothes from the dryer. We would move up, get into newer cars, we'd get a team, we'd find sponsors, and so on. We'd just won at Mason City, and Donnie had decided to spend the Fourth at home because the next month he'd be gone part of every week.

He and Walter wanted to go to our town's annual Demolition Derby and take J.P. He was old enough, they said. I backed out. I was tired, I told them, wanted time to just sit and go over the books on the salvage yard and talk to Mom. And I remember we all looked around at Mom like we'd forgotten she existed, and in a way I guess she had. She'd been disappearing so gradually, we hadn't noticed, not even Walter, though as I say that, I don't believe that part is true. Walter would have noticed. He just might not have been able to say anything. There she was, Mom, with this forced little smile on her thin face and her pale blue eyes so long gone you could tell they weren't seeing any of us sitting around the table of her house. She was already out the door, down the walk, past the heavy tire scallops of her fence, stepping into the UPS man's brand new Camaro, a too-good-to-be-true gold yellow. But I wouldn't see that for several more hours yet. You go ahead, she smiled. I'm fine. We can watch the fireworks from the garage roof and when you come home, we'll have some ice cream and beer.

It's the small lies we come to hold against a person, I've decided. Not that she wouldn't be there when they came home, that she'd leave me to face Walter by myself, but that she promised them ice cream she already knew she didn't have in the freezer. Ice cream and beer, that should've been a tip-off, don't you think?

Even her Ozarks hillbilly relatives knew better than to offer up a combination like that. What were we thinking, all of us?

So, like I said, when I came back from checking the books on the salvage yard, which Walter and Pugh did not bother keeping worth a darn, there was Mom packing. Wasn't much to say, really. At least I didn't try to say much. She was the determined one in our family, and she had that restlessness. I was a grown woman with a family of my own to worry about. I thought she'd be back, or that I'd go see her. I thought all kinds of things as I wrapped the glass swan in her underwear three, four times and bedded it safely with her socks on top of her jeans and put her T-shirts on top of that. I wasn't thinking about Walter. Her happiness swept all those thoughts up and away like a good strong wind blowing the house clean again as she opened the door and ran down to meet the yellow Camaro's honking horn. I carried the black nylon bag myself and put it in the trunk when he popped the lid, saw it safely resting on jumper cables next to a lava lamp even I knew was cheesy. His clothes were in a cardboard box. I remember a white athletic sock with a frayed heel hanging over the edge, and I reached to tuck it back in but stopped myself because suddenly I couldn't touch anything of his, as if his things were too nasty in a personal, naked way. I slammed the trunk lid and leaned down to kiss her goodbye, only getting the glance of her ear for she turned away too quickly to laugh at something he said. And by the time she turned back, he was stepping on the gas and spewing gravel from the tires that stung my bare legs as the car burst away, suddenly tearing a hole too big to be closed again.

Walter and Donnie and J.P. drove right by the wreck on their way home, hurrying to tell me about it. How they could still be excited by a wrecked car, I'll never know, but I didn't blame them, not at first. Not until they said it was a new yellow Camaro with the front end so crumpled they had to cut it in half to get the people out, and the rescue squad turned off the blinking lights after they loaded up the bodies. Kids, Walter said, and I couldn't look at him again for a month.

That was the end of our racing luck. I never understood how one thing got in the way of the other, and maybe it didn't, but maybe it did. We dug a hole of debt so deep we about drowned, and now even Walter's working twenty-four-seven to keep the bills at bay. We were all good to go, though in some strange way we didn't realize it, and then she went and took it away. So you know now that the remains of that Camaro are right inside the gate here where I can keep an eye on them. I never unpacked the trunk either, the one part of the car intact. I've left it there, the black nylon bag with the glass swan safely nestled in its dark sleep among her clothes. The UPS man's cardboard box molding and collapsing in the wet years since that dream arrived and took ahold of our lives. Because it's like Walter says, you pay for every mistake.

The Level of My Uncertainty

"I bet the whole family can weld." Someone always says something like that. Moving from track to track I've heard it all before. It's true that my wife Myna and three babies help out around the shop between competitions. Well, they aren't babies anymore. Dove is sixteen and she's the biggest help. She can hold a torch with the best of 'em. Tiny Pine, we call him T.P.—he's twelve and he's begging to get started driving on his own, soon as those legs of his grow. And even Cleo, the real baby at seven, is good at crawling into the engine cavity and wiring things that get to hanging loose.

All in all, a man couldn't wish for a better family, and the championship should have been mine, it should've. Everybody said it, not just the wife and kids who wear their pride on their faces and keep their disappoints in their hearts like I've taught 'em.

"A man is lucky to have a beautiful wife." That's the other thing people say about me. They don't know the half of it. With those looks, she can't help but produce a passel of kids I have to worry about taking after her. And they do. That Dove—well, and there's T.P. who's being followed around by every little girl on the lot, especially that clown Frogger's eleven year old who has red hair, for chrissakes, and is already five-eight. She's a giant. Why doesn't she pick on someone her own size? T.P. has life plans, not girl plans. Least that's what we tell each other as we work father and son, ripping torn metal sheets off and riveting new ones on the car each week. Thank goodness Cleo is still a baby, though she has her mama's brown curls and enough of Dove's big brown eyes to put a real scare into me. Dove, well, that will bear some thinking, I decide as I reinforce the gas tank on the '69 Olds I picked up last week from Fred's Salvage outside of Red Oak. The Olds is a tank, a big Ninety-Eight. Glance can run into me all day and I'll still be steering with my fingertips. They knew how to build 'em back then.

Dove saw that Olds. She thought I was buying it for her, maybe, from the hungry wishing look in her eyes. She's working inside the car right now, tearing out all the accessories. She finds that job more than satisfying and she is good at it to boot. She is the best stripper I know of and she can handle a torch like she's conducting a damn band. For a while there, when she was Tiny's age, she nagged me to let her start driving, but I put her off with one thing or another. Now I have to wonder if I made a mistake.

"There's Rhonda Harmon Smith running top-fuel dragsters," Dove said when she turned fourteen. Then a month ago, right there in the second week of school, she showed up at the garage and announced she was done. Not going back. Staying home to work on the cars with me. I knew what that was all about, but figured I'd let it ride a while. She'd get tired of the old man, but she hasn't.

And then the water man showed up twice last month. That got me to thinking for sure. Both times it was Dove left the shop, wiping her hands on a rag as she went into the office to sign the delivery slip and discuss God knows what because how hard could it be to lift one of those water bottles and set it upside-down in the holder for us? Myna was the mover and shaker behind the water deal. Said the well was tasting funny being so close to where we parked the old, demolished cars. I didn't wrangle. She's a beautiful woman, as I said, and a man learns early with such a wife to have a little give in him. And thinking on it, I began to notice that brake fluid aftertaste too, though you can't be sure in a deal like that.

The water man's driving up now, as I speak, pulling his white and blue truck around and looking in the side mirror to see if Dove is about. Well, I am a perverse son of a bitch, and I often have to stop myself for the general good of things. So I go over and thump on the roof of the car so she can hear me over the screeching and sawing racket she's making inside. She looks up startled, like our bird dog caught with its nose in the trash. It's not an expression I like to see. I tilt my head toward the water man's truck, and she glances that way and puts down the snippers and electric saw. She's getting to be a big girl, I notice as she climbs out and doesn't slam the door because she's busy smoothing herself down the way Myna does when she stands up to go to the bathroom all the way in the back corner of Black Charlie's down in Red Oak on a Thursday night.

I decide to watch. Like I have a choice, right?

She's wearing my old Doobie Brothers tee from the 1980 tour with the tear at the neck and washed so thin, well, you get the idea. I vow to use it to change the oil on the Olds soon as she takes it off. The water man has very strong, thick arms, lifting four bottles onto the dolly and easing them down the ramp while Dove stands there with her hands on her hips. I bet she's grinning. She who won't smile a whole day in the garage with me. Nor a whole long evening with the rest of us watching motor sports or tapes of the Derbies we've done well in. All the way to the championship a week ago. Should've won, like I said. Radiator puncture. What's the luck of that, you ask, but I have my family with me. We travel in that old camper, roasting hot dogs and marshmallows over the barbeque I made from an oil pan and a Chevy grill. Handy as you please.

The water man spends a long time unloading today. Off where I don't dare go and see because she'll know what I'm doing. I work real quiet repacking the bearings on Seidel's car he left this morning, my back just a few feet from the office door which we keep open to hear the phone. Once I missed a chance at an interview with ESPN2 keeping the door shut, so now, you know, a person needs the boost once in while. It's not easy climbing in those cars every week, getting smashed around all afternoon, hoping to come out with enough money to take the family to a good sit-down dinner that night. It's not all fun and games. That's what I would've told them. They caught me at the track just before the second qualifier at the Championships, and we had a few good words, but it's not the same as being featured. I could use a sponsor, I mean I sponsor myself, of course, the garage, but it's becoming more a team deal now, and I just have the family.

What's taking so long in there? This is the tricky part. A man doesn't want to push on his sixteen-year-old daughter, and Dove has never—she's good with that torch. She can gut an engine faster than you can say Jack Sprat, and she's never—she comes home at night. That water man looks older, a lot I mean.

What does a man have to do?

Last night we were watching a rerun of that last Winston Cup race at Rockingham and Dove starts in about steering boxes, ratios of turning, tire pyrometers and depth gages, and which cars picked up a push and which ones were getting loose. It scared me. I looked over at Myna and she lifted her eyebrows as if to say she didn't know either. We're a Demolition Derby family, I wanted to remind her. We have a tradition here. Not many can say that. But I didn't. I watched Dove's eyes taking in the fancy matched outfits the pit crews were wearing, down to the expensive metallic stripe shoes, and the hustle they used shooting that jackhammer around and changing tires, taping and riveting after someone kissed the wall, squirting fuel into the tanks and letting it splash out without a care in the world as the driver peeled off. Her heart was right there, I could tell, and she wasn't bothering to hide it.

She's laughing some more. I lie down on my creeper, slide under the car, and angle myself so I can see through the open door of the office. Really, I am not trying to spy. But she is my daughter, my only Dove, and she could weld a house in a hurricane if you asked her to.

The water man is drinking water from one of those paper cones they dispense right next to the bottle. Dove is turning the spigot on and off fast enough to catch a drop or two at a time on her finger and licking it and he's watching and they're laughing at nothing. Absolutely nothing that I can see. His dolly is standing there with the empties loaded on. And he's wearing cowboy boots. You'd think his feet would get tired. Mine do. I tried, when I was a younger man and courting a beautiful woman, to wear those boots everywhere, but I had to give it up after I crushed my ankles that time in Omaha. I knew the Chevy was too light. Pure luck I survived as long as I did. Damn Crazy Eddie had a Cadillac big as a hearse. It probably *was* an old hearse, now that I think of it. Took the front end of my Chevy and practically shoved it up my nose. Hurt like the dickens. End of my boots and dancing days. Now Myna has to dance with others while I watch. Early in the evening it's other women she knows, wives and girlfriends from the Sears where she works in Automotive. Well, why not, she could rebuild an engine any time she had a mind to, but she's in sales not service. Later, as things get louder, the men get braver and ask her to dance, with little sideways looks at me. I nod as if to say, you go ahead, go right ahead, but she always goes home with me. I used to drink a little too much those nights, but I don't anymore.

As long as I'm under this thing, might as well change the oil, surprise Seidel, he's too cheap to ask for it. Funny thing about that run last week. When I hauled the car back home, got the radiator patched, and turned it on, the engine froze up solid. No oil.

I pull the oil plug and let it drain out in a thick black ooze. Seidel's lucky he's got an engine left.

What's she doing? He's sitting on the edge of my desk, and she's standing between his legs. That's not right. She's got her hands on the water man's thighs, resting there. That's definitely not right. I push myself out toward the door, but she steps back and he stands before I have a chance. She's shaking her head and picking at her fingernails, looking like a kid being asked to get in the car by a stranger. I'm thinking of going in there, but she turns and gives the spigot of that water bottle a good yank, splashing water out in a wasteful stream. That's not what's worrying me though. The water man touches her long braid, his face not looking like a stranger's. But he's not cruel in the way his fingers stroke the straight thick brown hair she has inherited from me and my people. It stops me. I have seen my own hand at such a gesture with my wife. I know it for what it is. There is longing in this water man as he speaks to my daughter. And there is longing in the hand she reaches out for him, the hand I have seen so ferociously gutting wires and hoses and upholstery all morning long, so that now it is nicked and dirty, but full of its own promise nonetheless.

I wonder if she loosened the nuts on my car's oil pan last Sunday, and made the engine freeze up. I suppose if she drove the screwdriver through the grill herself, draining the water, it is the least I could give her.

My whole family can weld, and we often do, a team making the thick, protective seams on the cars I am wrecking. After Dove, T.P. will be next, then little Cleo the baby who at seven still nestles on my beautiful wife's lap in the shade of the awning I've salvaged and rigged along the side of the camper for my family.

I was running good that day, won the first qualifier, only had minor repairs to make for the second. I suppose it was Dove on the engine, tidying up. I guess I can picture her there, now that I think on it. I was in the zone, that's what everybody was saying. I'm no Dale Jarrett, but I was on the money. Driving into the ring, the Pontiac engine chugging and roaring, a little lift there to the right side where Homer had run into us hard last go, I looked around, ready to take every last one of them down. Before the flag dropped, I saw Dove standing there on the sidelines, arms crossed, not waving like the rest of them. In fact, she wasn't even looking at me, I realize now. Her head was turned, looking directly into the sun at something the other side of her, squinting and frowning. If I could, knowing what I know at this moment, I guess I'd get out of that car and run over to her there on the side-lines. Leave the engine running, sure, just climb out and take a hike over the dirt bank and bales of straw and stand there next to my daughter and see what it is she's seen that is taking her that way, not this.

And then the radiator went.

So I replace the filter and gasket, wipe the plug down and tighten the whole thing. Scoot out and pour the new oil in. One of the real pleasures of life is the butterscotch stream arcing into that hole. I can't even say why, but it makes me feel good to see that every time. I screw the cap on and check the oil level, wiping the old dip off on my coveralls first. The new read is clear and full, and I rub my fingers in the oil just because it's what I do. Like I deserve it. I haven't looked up the whole time, you understand. Not once. I keep my back to them, protecting all of us.

Over the Point of Cohesion

That was the strange thing. He woke up thinking he'd been right on it going into that corner, so he hadn't braked. But he'd been wrong, stepped on the brakes too late and took the wall. Just like that. But he'd been so sure. Then the long stay in the hospital getting rehab and listening to people congratulate him for his twelfth year and this special award for his retirement and being a good sport so he could stand on the stage in New York with the top ten. Well, standing wasn't exactly right. It took him a whole year just to stagger along with those metal braces, and he'd never stand without the odd bend to his back, swaying him to one side like a tree pushed by the wind. None of that mattered.

He looked up at the waitress pouring the coffee like it was some grand achievement and then went back to scribbling numbers on the napkin. He'd made the drawing of the track at Martinsville, the angles of the corners, written what he remembered of the setup on the car, and began rebuilding the race in his mind. Some days it was the race he'd run. Some days it was the race he was going to run, and some days it was the race he should've run. Those were the hardest days, when he corrected each move, each brake and throttle, each bump at the rear or side of the other cars. But never that corner. He'd gone in right. He knew it. He couldn't believe it hadn't worked out. He'd demanded the printouts from the team in the pit and gotten them. But they didn't show enough, he'd protested, and the men looked away. Twelve years and they couldn't look him in the eye.

"Anything else?"

"What?"

"Anything else for you?"

He looked up at her to see if he could figure out what it was made her need to bother him like this. The waitresses usually left him alone of a morning. They had plenty to do without nagging him. She was plain. Plain brown hair, plain brown eyes, prim little lips with caked pink lipstick her tongue kept finding. By the end of her shift her lips would be chapped. He knew that because he'd had the same problem racing and had to coat his lips with balm before he packed himself into the helmet. He shook his head. "Just leave the pot, okay?"

"Can't. I'll be back." She disappeared and left him alone for so long he began to worry he was going to have to order more coffee. Another thing he could do now. Couldn't afford the nerves or the dehydration before. Now—

He held up his cup finally, and she took her time while he anxiously searched the cafe. He didn't see anyone he knew, but that was probably because he hadn't made it a point to make friends when he'd moved here eight months ago. He wasn't even sure why he chose this place, but it seemed far enough away that he wouldn't miss what he was missing every moment of his day. Iowa. Nebraska. Kansas. He'd gone down the list of places far enough away from his racetracks to be safe. Kansas. Hays. Out there on the plains, his eye taking in the wheatfields like they were the prime surfaces of newly poured concrete with just enough skin over so the tires didn't shred up like at North Wilksboro. Last race a week ago. Opened in 1949, he'd been there five times himself. Never won. Hardly ever in top ten, hell, top twenty. Hell, it wasn't his deal, the short tracks. Something nagged at him. Okay, maybe he wasn't any Rusty Wallace or Richard Petty and that new kid, Gordon, who might be the best of them all. Even Dale Earnhardt couldn't take it away from him, running second at North Wilksboro, bridesmaid to the bride again. That would chap old Dale's ass. But he came back. After his last pileup, Dale came back and raced with a broken collarbone.

She took his cup and poured the coffee and stood there, looking at him. Her eyes weren't so dull brown, he noticed, every once in a while there was a little spark of purple or blue-black like what he saw when he closed his eyes sometimes, like a movie trying to get started, but having trouble with the reel. She kept staring, pot held up like a trophy in both hands. He looked away again, still nobody he knew. Half farmers, half cowboys in their straw hats and boots, spending more time than he'd ever had sitting in the cafe at the Sunoco. Outside in the parking lot, the bawls of cattle in the long silver stock trucks and the tires whishing on the interstate two blocks away. Every sound carried on the plains where the wind blew almost nonstop and it was like an ocean that sank him deep into sleep every night, that wash of engines and tires. Sometimes the way he'd heard it in his car during a race, only much quieter, safer, under control, rarely the winding engine, the screeching metal on metal.

"What are you?" She gestured with the pot toward the napkins he'd written on.

He had the urge to climb out of the booth and leave, but it wasn't time yet so he shrugged.

"You don't know what you are?" She grinned and looked back at the counter where the manager was talking head to head with a bleached blonde whose body had seen better days. His waitress put the coffeepot down on the table and leaned her fists tiredly on the edge as if to reassure him she wasn't going to claim more than that little bit of space.

"You're new, just move here?" She fingered the drawing of the corner where it happened.

"Been here a while, few months."

"Just learning those things, huh." She tipped her head toward the metal braces on his legs he kept propped up on the bench opposite him. His legs ached almost all the time, and raising them seemed to keep the pain at more of a distance. It'd taken a long time to pry them apart from the metal and engine. Almost too long, the doc said after they'd saved the things. "Saved the legs," he'd announced after surgery. "Don't have to worry about that." His sponsors had sent him flowers, fruit baskets, and farewell checks. There'd been talk of a benefit dinner or concert to help him, but he'd never returned the phone calls. Just moved here, a place he'd found on the interstate, far enough away.

She looked over her shoulder again as the manager slipped out the double glass front doors and turned the corner with the blonde who still had very nice legs. The waitress looked at him and made a scooting gesture with her hands, and he pulled his feet off the bench, hating the clunk each foot made when it hit the tired brown linoleum beneath the table.

"Thanks. Feels good to take a load off. Dennis won't be back for a while. He goes down to this other place. Has his morning coffee there. That's his girlfriend. His ex-wife. They keep at it, gotta give them that." She pushed the thin brown hair off her forehead with the back of her hand and looked around. "That's Frank up there at the end of the counter, he comes in almost every morning on his way to Salina, hauling cattle for some big place out by Colby. He's never been further east than Kansas City, doesn't like anyplace he hasn't been, he says. And Johannes there in the hat with the feather? He was a rodeo cowboy in high school, went on the circuit, got stomped on too hard by a bull in Tulsa, Oklahoma and lost the retina of one eye. Sees fine for farming, but he don't drive so good. Nobody dares say a word. I went to school with him. And that guy there—"

He stopped listening. It was too much like the obituaries. He didn't subscribe to the racing news anymore either. It isn't over till it's over, he kept telling himself. If he could figure out how that corner turned into a slingshot and put his car into that wall, well, then maybe.

"You're hanging onto the wrong things," his wife had said as she packed. She hadn't even taken the bank account, what there was of it, and he'd felt that as a kind of double insult. Hell, she hadn't even slammed the door behind her when the cab honked out front, like in those country songs. But it hadn't been a cab. It was a friend of hers from work. She'd had to hold down a job those last three years to pay the mortgage because he was on such a shoestring, they couldn't keep a house that size and the two cars and all without her paycheck. "Soon as I start winning again," he'd promised her, but after those early years when he was young and full of vinegar, there hadn't been much.

"Head injury?" the waitress asked all of a sudden.

He examined her face to see if she was making fun of him, but she wasn't. "I—" He couldn't say it. He hadn't said it yet, wouldn't till he understood how that car had failed him.

"My brother and cousin died in a car wreck out County Road 4, the year I was up at Chadron State, north of here? Massive head injuries. Closed casket. Mom hated that part. Almost as much as losing Lonnie, I think. Saying goodbye to your loved ones and all that stuff. Very important. You had a car wreck too?"

He nodded.

"Thought so. You're still not used to them leg thingies. And the scars on your arms and face there. I noticed that. Part of my training." She waved at the room. "Not this, I'm saving to go back to school. Mortuary science."

His stomach filled up something nasty. What did she want?

"Lonnie wanted to be a drag racer. He and Jackie were practicing, something went wrong, and they crashed into each other going a hundred and ten. I didn't know that old car of his would go that fast. Guess he'd been working on the engine. Anyways—" She twisted her hands together and back apart.

"Hard business to make a living in. Most people don't make it," he said and shifted his legs in their metal cages to move the aches around.

"How old do you think I am?" she asked suddenly, smiling at him in a way that took the coarse grain out of her skin and made her seem younger than he'd thought.

He shrugged.

"No, take a guess. Really—"

"Thirty, thirty-five?" He'd made a mistake. The light died in her eyes and she pushed back against the burgundy Naugahyde of the booth. "I'm no good at that—I never—"

She looked toward the counter and waved her fingers at him. "Never mind."

It made him feel something, bad maybe, and he didn't like it. "No, look, what's your name? I'm—" He'd been about to give her the name he'd earned his rookie year, Spit, but he didn't want to do that, not now, not yet. "My name's Ricky, Ricky Torrence."

She swallowed, brushed her hair off her face, and looked at him quickly, then at the cuticle she was picking. "Bonnie Jassy." She smiled again. "Bonnie and Lonnie—my parents—"

They sat there uncomfortably for a few moments, then she pulled the napkin with the drawing on it around again, looked at it, and shoved it back at him. "So what's this?"

"Racetrack."

"The rest of this stuff racing too?" Her fingers touched a couple of the other napkins lightly, with enough respect that he nodded. "You a racecar person?"

"Driver."

"What kind?"

"Winston Cup." He wanted to look away when he said it, but he found himself staring at her face which changed again, lighting up as he remembered women's had in the racing days. It still made him feel good, and he pinched the thigh his hand was resting on to punish the thought.

"Lonnie mostly watched the dragsters, funny cars, straight line stuff. So I never got to see you, I guess."

"It doesn't matter."

She looked at the scars on his arms and face where they'd sewn him back together, and he got ready for the questions. "Crashed, huh?"

It always made him feel like he'd committed some big social mistake, a crime even, that he'd messed up enough to earn exile from all human decency by crashing into that wall, the sponsor decals crumpling, then flying pieces in the air, miraculously inflicting only minor injuries in the crowd while he tumbled and turned and torqued down the racetrack, taking out five other cars in the process. The race leaders who were lapping him for the fourth time. Hell, he hadn't even been on the lead lap, he woke up thinking. What was the glory of a crash like his?

"They start you small in school and work up to crash victims. I skipped ahead in the textbook and read that part first."

"Hit the wall going 118 at Martinsville." Suddenly he found himself talking, telling her every detail of the race as if she were just dying to hear it, and he knew he was acting crazy, not letting her into the conversation, holding her attention captive at gunpoint, as his wife used to say, but he couldn't stop himself and she kept nodding and smiling like she understood exactly what he was saying and it was utterly fascinating.

"At Martinsville, you need to be careful of brakes, see. We use carbon-metallic brakes that heat up to a thousand degrees until they're glowing red and sparking. You have to be careful because eventually they can melt the bead that seals the rubber of your tire to the wheel. Some of the teams were starting to use metallic tape to prevent the bead from melting, but we didn't, we didn't think we needed it with the setup on the car and me driving. I wasn't hard on the brakes, most of the time. Hell, I wasn't going fast enough to be hard, I guess." It surprised him saying that.

"So what happened on this corner?" She tapped the drawing.

He took a sip of the cold coffee and made a little face but she ignored him. In fact, she had her chin propped with her two fists and was staring right at him, full force. "What happened?"

He shook his head. "There's this point of cohesion on a corner. You hit it and you don't have to brake so much, you go over it and you have to brake hard. Simple. Somehow the car got loose on me. I thought it was running a little tight and when I got there, it was loose and I was kissing the wall. It made the highlights tape on all the networks, and the year-end film for the awards banquet." He didn't mention the video of the worst wrecks of the decade they were selling on late night TV when they reran old races for the diehard fans. Somehow that embarrassed him.

"Must've been something." She shook her head and looked at the pieces of napkin, letting her eyes slide to the counter again. He pretended not to notice.

"It was. I've been trying to figure out what happened, how it happened. But it doesn't show up in the numbers like it should. Nobody tapped me or nothing. I don't know." He shook his head and the numbers jiggled on the paper in front of him. Sometimes his vision did that.

"Pretty obvious, isn't it, Ricky?" She stood and picked up the coffeepot as the manager came through the glass doors looking around with a critical expression ready to accuse somebody of something.

"How's that?" He felt the bile climbing in his chest. Acid reflux, not your heart, it's strong as an ox, the doctor at the clinic on the other side of downtown had told him last week.

"You made a mistake," she said and spilled a little more coffee into his cup before she left.

"Yeah," he agreed. But it should show up somehow, shouldn't it? What was the point of all that printout business if it didn't tell the story when you needed it? Maybe he'd explain more of the details to Bonnie tomorrow, he decided. Maybe by doing that, he'd find the thing he'd been missing in all that data. Then he stopped himself. Mortuary science? What kind of a job was that? He had to stop himself from calling out the question to the whole room.

The Pop Off Valve

Men always tell me their sex secrets. So it was a relief, you see, when all Bobby had to confess was this thing he had for cars. How hard could that be? And after one thing and another, we got married. Didn't take but a little bit of time. Or as Bobby likes to point out, an Indy car can cover a football field in one second, so everything's relative, right?

And I didn't mind the honeymoon at the Motor Speedway in Irish Hills. Michigan, well, the pretty part's up north, you know, but I was in that giving mood marriage starts out in. I gave him my truck for the trip down. I gave him my jacket when the weather suddenly turned raw and nasty and I could see he was the kind of man who wouldn't know what to pack for a trip. And I gave him my heart when a driver he liked crashed in the timed pole laps. We were standing there, beside the fence, as I would see him do later with our kid on the football field, his hands gripping cold metal the whole time, while the rescue workers used the jaws of life to pry what was left of the driver from the shattered burnt shell of the car.

We grilled steaks on the hibachi at dark, unable to see the bloody raw meat until we cut into it and ate it anyway, what we could of it, because it was too late to do anything else. The beers didn't change the smell of burning paint and flesh that hung over the racetrack all afternoon as a sad reminder of what our infield tickets had bought and paid for. I thought then that he might let

Taking the Wall   37

go of it, this thing he had for cars, that he would see how world-discouraging races can be for those on the sidelines. Take up golf maybe. That's as much and as little as I knew then.

It's fifteen years later, and the son we made at dawn in that camper shell, the truck springs rocking in the early quiet before the roar and rumble of motors took over, is out shooting baskets or tossing the football with his friends. It's Sunday, and for years that has meant not the crowd roar of football games, but the rhythmic whine of racecars weaving in and out along the track on their high-low drive lines.

Last night while I waited to trap him into bed, Bobby told me there are four thousand parts in an Indy car engine, and few if any gaskets. His eyes had that distant moon-gazing look that I always associate with the dog just before it starts barking at the stars.

Lately at work, Ron has been making little moves. You know the ones, the brush of an arm against the side of your breasts, the reaching of a hand to take the lint off your shoulder, the extra smiles and semidirty cartoons at your station. He's not in automotive. That's one thing you can say for him. He's in housewares. His days spent inspecting the shelves of Rubbermaid containers, laundry soap, and electric brooms. Ron isn't bad looking. His hair reaches back, not forward, but at least he doesn't wrap it around his head like some crazy stitching on a baseball. When he rolls up his sleeves to restock, his forearms are thick and corded with veins and muscles the way I like. See, I admitted it. Just a few days ago, Ron came by and told me he'd once been with a Catholic nun from Traverse City. His grin reminded me so much of my boy joking about underwear. She was on a trial run from the order, Ron confessed. A fifty-year-old virgin. Even he looked astonished at the notion, and tapped the back of my hand with his fingers.

He's using Sen-Sen and working up to something, you can tell. His new jeans are a size tighter. You can see from the label, and, well, from the back when he walks away. Although I have never been a woman given to looking at men's behinds, I can understand the urge. Ron has nice long legs too. It makes me wonder if he wears cowboy boots in his off hours. He looks like the kind of man who'd do that, whether he had a horse or not, and I get a little lift under my rib cage thinking about it.

Bobby's worried about the year-end points. The Championships in all the divisions except Busch cars are close this year. He spends the evenings he's not watching the kid practice or play in a game working on the numbers with the TV turned to the races he's taped since he can't watch them all on Sunday. We have four TVs in the house. One for each person and the dog, I guess. Each with its own VCR, and I still can't watch anything on the weekends. Toss up, he says. Honda-Lola on Firestone or Ford-Reynard on Goodyear. With Indy cars, it's the battle of tires and engines. With Winston Cup cars, it's Chevy or Pontiac or Ford. I know just by looking now what the crisis is, what the battle will shape up to be. I know so much useless information, I'm embarrassed just opening my mouth some days at work. The other day at lunch break when Ron told me about the ex-girlfriend who set fire to his garage, I couldn't think of anything to say but, "the lower you go, the more Gs you put on." We both looked at me stunned.

Not that Bobby isn't a good provider. I read those columns in the papers, and I can see I have nothing to complain about. One kid is good enough. We probably couldn't afford more without Bobby having to add to the route, take on weekends or evenings. Bad enough during the holidays when they think nothing of asking him for all sorts of extra hours. Being a UPS delivery man though, he gets to wear uniforms so clothes aren't ruined at work, and sometimes he gets Shopper's City on his route and we sneak off for a quick bite together. He doesn't want much in life. He's not an expensive bass boat or motorcycle kind of guy. We saved for the satellite dish together and made it count for three years worth of presents. It was fun, like the old days, keeping track of spare change and forgoing movies and nights out so we could save. It always brought a smile to Bobby's face when we added a few more dollars on Friday night, and we often as not ended up in bed early, fooling around.

Afterwards, we'd lie there naked side by side, the covers tangled on the floor, and talk about how we got together so easily. Like a good engine, our parts met and knew each other from the first time we said hello. Sometimes we'd remember the honeymoon week in Irish Hills at the races and talk about the other people we met, like the group of firemen who traveled in a big Winnebago all the way from Omaha, and the old couple who had come racing for the last thirty years. They slept one in front, one in back, in their big white '65 Cadillac. With only a couple of rust puckers, the car was nearly mint, and they always got offers and they always turned them down. Those nights in bed we remembered so much detail from that trip, it was enough to make me weep, because anymore I can't remember one day from the next. Can't tell you what I did aside from work, what I ate, or who I talked to. There is a time, I've come to understand, when everything you do is new, and it never lasts long enough, and it never can be recalled without dimming the present a little more, like an electrical short drawing too much power off the engine.

Sometimes on those nights, I confess, I asked Bobby for a sex secret. He'd study the question, you could see it in the way he lifted his hand and turned it over and over in the dim light from the hallway, his wedding ring a dull glint in the dark. He couldn't even make one up, you see, that's how Bobby is. Once he rolled over on me and whispered that in an Indy 500 race, the engines go through 2.2 million individual piston strokes, and I kept seeing those shining pistons rising and plunging in their hot shining holes as he made me moan under him.

His favorite driver's using a 1994 chassis with a '96 Mercedes engine, Bobby tells me at breakfast this morning. I have to go in because Mauricia is sick again, and they have no backup with Bill already out, I tell him. We'd had waffles, the good kind, in the toaster oven, with maple flavored syrup, he and I. The boy is still sleeping. All he does is sleep and eat and run around at night, but I'm only jealous, I tell myself. He's a good kid. Bobby is watching the Indy race, not the Winston Cup or trucks, because it's coming down to the wire now.

Packing fresh kleenex and lipstick in my purse, I watch Bobby at the kitchen table, in his son's Party Naked! T-shirt and pajama bottoms. He has the sports sections of three papers spread out around him, comparing stories and complaining about the lack of motor sports coverage in general. Thank God for television, he mutters. He keeps his brown hair short, in a crew cut almost, except it falls forward into a v on his forehead like some little kid, and he's chewing his fingernail. He only allows himself one to really chew on, the others he just clips with his teeth. He has that kind of will, you see, that's why I don't bother mentioning the piles of pale quarter moons he leaves on tables around the house.

When I open the door, he looks up surprised and pleased as if I am just arriving, not leaving. This is also the expression he wears at the start of every race when the afternoon is all possibility and promise as the cars zigzag their way down the track toward the starting flag, bringing heat up into the cold tires. By the time I return in the evening, the race will be over, and, often as not, it will be another tale of woe that greets me, how a pit stop under green cost his favorite driver the race or an engine blew on the final lap. If only they can wait till the yellow caution flags are out, I pray as I close the door, but I don't want anyone to get hurt. Maybe a puff of smoke and all skate, but no explosions, no cars hurtling through the air at the spotters and crowds along the fence. No crashes, please, that end anything. Because that's what I'm going to tell Ron today, you can't rev to the top of your range for very long and expect to make 500 miles. You need to pay attention to your pop off valve and back off before it goes. Maybe I should be saying this to Bobby instead, I don't know, but I will in a while, won't I?

Omaha

We're sitting around waiting for the rain to make up its mind, playing Omaha. Rooster deals the four cards down and we all bet. Henry, the transport driver, is on short call in case the track washes out and Fat Fred is all that's left of the pit crew. The others have gone back to their camper with a two-way in case it clears. They've driven half the night to make the show here in Michigan after putting in a full day at work. So it's the four of us, and I raise it by two, and Rooster puts three cards up in the middle for everyone to bet on. It busts my flush, but lo and behold I start on a damn high straight that looks pretty good. Rooster is the best player, but as the crew chief he'd have to have that kind of cool. Carl, the owner, beeps again, and we all stop and look outside the garage at the dripping sky. The weather has scrubbed the face off things pretty good, and the track shines like Black Beauty for a few minutes, if you don't remember the cracks and bumps that'll send cars into the wall today. If the damn sun ever comes out.

Doc, our driver, is in his motor home like always, sleeping or screwing around with his computer. He has to stay local now, Carl ruled after Daytona when Doc snuck off to town and got himself tattoos of his car number thirty-three in big sunbursts on both shoulders. Hurt him enough in the fire suit that he had trouble making the turns. "That was a dumbass kid thing to do,"

Carl had yelled. "Well, he *is* a dumbass kid," Rooster had muttered, and we all knew the truth of that. But it was Rooster got Doc on the internet and now all we have to worry about on race days is how pink the kid's eyes are from staying up all night talking to his girlfriend in Romania. We already lug five hundred pounds of weights around in case the kid needs to work out. Got that idea from Mark Martin. Doc's not even thirty, he can live on HoHo's and ice cream bars and still not have to worry about zipping the jump suit up the middle. Sometimes I wish he'd go with the Jesus boys and spend his free time on his knees. Or get married. Time for Doc to settle down. We've all been saying that. Then maybe he'd be grateful to sit around the garage playing this damn card game he's taught us.

Everybody's in. Rooster deals a single card up for everyone and the betting starts again at a leisurely pace. We're in no big damn hurry. We got chips and coke and cards. While we're waiting for Fat Fred to make up his mind picking up and setting down his cards fifty times like they might change once they have time to think things through on the table again, we all look out the garage doors. The rain has stopped dripping and now we're waiting for the track to dry. Pretty soon they'll have the trucks and blowers out there. Since we've already gone out and tried to run once, we can't touch the cars. Swaps is sitting there under the cover next to us, and it's like he can't wait to get out there. Sometimes I swear I can feel his headlight decals staring right through my back, trying to grab my lungs in his teeth and force me to let him out of here. You're going soon enough, I tell him in my head. I wouldn't be in any big hurry with Doc at the reins. We're lucky to finish a race, let alone have a car whole enough to drive itself onto the transport. Last week on the way to Pocono, Secretariat broke loose in the carrier and smashed his nose in. Had to replace the radiator just to be safe. Great idea naming these things after racehorses. Doc again. He's a piece of brilliance. Got his name from some radio show, Doctor Science. He's always trying to come up with new ideas for the car, things like using Velcro on the windshield to make it easier to replace. Yeah, that'd be safe. He's not a bad kid.

It'd be nice to have a driver like Rusty Wallace or Daryl Waltrip. Somebody with some smarts could help you when things got rough in qualifying or Happy Hour. He'll learn, Rooster says. But I'm still thinking about that experiment he ran at home with us a month ago. He'd seen it on the Home Improvement Channel, which I don't really believe exists. Taped off five sections of oil-stained cement where we worked on the cars and poured coke on one part, then bleach and soap and some other chemicals he'd picked up on each of the others. The idea was to see which cleaned best, but he'd managed to get ahold of some kind of acid that spilled over the masking tape lines and interacted with the other things and sent us choking out of there as fast as we could go. There was a hole in the floor when the firefighters got through. Carl held us responsible for that one. Said we should know better than to let the kid play around with toxic materials. I haven't felt the same about Coca-Cola since.

Shoot. Rooster gives us one more card up. Three of us have possible straights showing so mine's worth zip. What the hell is this? Carl the owner buzzes in again. Rooster nods as if Carl can see him, then says, "Okay," and tosses in a ten-dollar bill. He clicks off and we all bet. Out of all these cards I have to find two in my hand and three in the middle that add up to something in this game called Omaha. Fat Freddy takes no time at all which is not good. Henry who never talks or does anything but hold the unlit cigarette in his teeth, grimaces and folds. It's up to me. High or High-Low. I've got nothing to speak of, but damn if I'm going to let Rooster or Fat Freddy get away without a run for their money. Behind me the car sighs and creaks.

Everybody's talking about how nice it'd be if NASCAR let us put computers in the cars so Winston Cup would have telemetry like Indy cars. Sure, get some bio-cam on the driver too. Like at Charlotte when the blower hose came off and was spewing hot air in Doc's face for a hundred laps. He was cooking in there, but he never said a word over the radio except during the fourth caution when he said that maybe they could think about putting air conditioning in the cars this summer before it got really hot.

Cars cost a hundred grand now, and we couldn't afford to go racing if the cost went up much more. Besides, shouldn't the driver have to do something?

If I could just go Low, I could maybe take it, but with this damn game, you have to take both High and Low. Rooster ignores Doc's callback for a minute to watch me with those big cow brown eyes behind the wire rim glasses. Reason he's Rooster is the crowing he makes when his team does well. Fast pit, good setup on the car, pole position, or win. It's been a while since any of us heard it though, and his gray hair says he's not getting any younger. The loudspeaker announces that the track's drying now, the front has moved on through. Not expecting another one till dark. Time enough to get the race in. There's ESPN to consider, the television crew pulling the plastic sheets off the cameras as the big blower trucks inch down the track side by side. Pretty soon they'll ask us to pull the cars out, drive around. With the headers pouring 1,200 degrees onto the track when they're starting, and 1,800 degrees when they're full out, the surface dries damn fast.

"Okay, okay." I fold the cards face down and shove my chair back a couple of inches so I'm nearer the car. Around the time Doc fires the engine and rolls onto the track he's going to ask us which of the identical thirty-threes he's in, and like always, we're going to say, "it's your favorite, Swaps, the fastest." Then he's going to wait half a lap before he says, "wasn't that what you said last week?"

There'll be lots of green-flag racing today, because at Michigan you can run three wide in places. It's a fast track with easy passing. If Doc's on, he can run 200 MPH into turn one and still finish the race. Just has to watch his fuel and turn three. It's one of the places we use the cold air box. But he has to watch going into turn three and letting the car drift up and lean against the wall of air there. Then there's the setup. If the sun comes out, the track changes, and I'll be sticking spring rubbers in and pulling them out all afternoon.

Rooster has a straight flush. Son of a damn gun. He takes our money in one handy swipe and it disappears. Henry leans back and almost tips the chair over, catching his cowboy boot heel against the leg of my chair just in time. He lifts the team hat and resettles it, his cigarette half-damp with spit bounces up and down in his grin. "Another game?" Fat Freddy says, but Rooster shakes his head and glances at the TV set we're using for the Weather Channel. Later we'll move it outside and keep it tuned to the race while we listen to the spotters and the radio. I'm doing the fuel mileage today, so I have all my charts and calculations ready. All week I've tried to explain it to Doc, about running leaner and taller, not using the engine so hard, but making sure he keeps enough fuel in the engine so it doesn't burn up. He's not a bad kid, if the other drivers would leave him alone. It's his rookie year, and they're testing him every step of the way. Can he take it, is he patient, can they put him in the wall every race until he's so sick of it or we're so sick of it he disappears back into dirt tracks?

We all stand up and Henry takes custody of the cards. Fat Freddy trots off to call the pit crew and Rooster walks out to meet Carl coming down from the owners' meeting. I'm the one lifts the cover from Swaps and peers inside the dark to see how he's feeling. Everything smells good in there—oil, paint, and the wet metal scent of new welding. There's the picture of Einstein with the wild hair on the dash. We'll have to take it off if he ever gets the on-board camera, but for now, it makes the kid happy to think we think there's a connection. The seat looks inviting but I know it's not an invitation I'll ever take. My job is making springs, putting shocks in, taking care of the chassis and engine, fuel and tires. I pat the window frame and notice the attachment on the window net is coming loose. Have to fix that, can't have the kid falling out on his head before he wins his first race for us.

Maybe things are beginning to look up. Last week it was Earnhardt himself, the Intimidator, who said, "I stuck my nose out there, I probably coulda drilled him a couple of times—" But he'd gone on and let Doc run ahead of him a couple of laps until the right rear tire started going down and we tried pulling the kid in, but the rear end tore loose and he spun like a damn ballerina up and away, tapped the wall lightly, then floated down into the grass. He was damn proud of himself saving the car as much as he did, and not taking anyone else with him. For once I had to agree and thank Earnhardt. See, we told each other, there is hope. And that was with only one roof flap working to slow the car so it wouldn't go airborne. Heck, with two working, who knew what was possible. You see, no matter how many times we go over the car, there's always something doesn't work. Look at those Yates engines blowing up for a month until they realized they couldn't just replace the broken or worn parts. Now it's Rusty Wallace's turn. And even with on-board computers, those Indy cars break down. Nothing is completely predictable.

I can hear Doc whistling as he comes in the garage looking new as a kid starting school. His sandy hair is buzz cut like the boys are doing now. No moustache, nothing but that corn-fresh face and the kind of reflexes an astronaut could envy.

"I have an idea—" he starts in, and I nod, bending to find the tools I need for the window net. You see, he's not a bad kid, with his big restless hands touching the car, the tools, the back of the chair Henry was tipping back in. They're like two big pale moths, lunas I believe they're called. This morning there was one as big as the palm of my hand clamped to the screen window of my motel room. We stared at each other, both of us stuck there by the rain pouring off the eaves in a straight silver curtain onto the broken cement walk. It seems silly somehow to trust all our futures in those hands, I think as I tighten the clamp and test the net again and again. After a few laps today he'll get racy like all the youngsters do, but he mustn't get hurt, he must ride as safe as we can make him.

It's true that in racing you either win or you lose. Usually you don't think of the third thing, but there is one. An excluded middle. It's Omaha, where you don't go racing, where you do nothing but wait and work and wait while it rains and dries and rains some more. It's what you do in between times that takes up most of your life.

What's It Take?

"Adultery doesn't run in my family either," Sonny told her, hefting the last tire onto the truck bed. A scuff he'd picked up at Michigan Speedway the week before, it joined three others he was pretending were a matched set from Dale Jarrett's 88 Quality Care Ford.

Lauralee stood there, arms crossed, straight red hair framing her long face, watching him with those jack-o'-lantern eyes like it was him had stayed out till dawn, not her. "You don't like me." Her voice was flat as pavement. She'd gotten out of the car at the end of the block, and if he hadn't already been loading for the trip to the dirt track in Bentonville, he wouldn't have seen her. And her lame ass excuse would've held up. Might've, he reminded himself, lifting the sprung tailgate and slamming it hard enough to make the rusty hookums catch.

"Where're you going?" she asked, her tone softer than before when she'd been defending herself against the way he looked right through her.

He lifted the old red and yellow Pennzoil cap and resettled it, but the little breeze couldn't move his greasy brown hair off his neck. He never showered before the track, not even in the old days when he was the hot, young, sprint driver. Bad luck to bathe then. Now it was important to look like if he didn't have bad luck, he wouldn't have any luck at all. Helped get and sell stuff.

Lauralee stepped out of her white high heels, pushed them away with the side of her foot, and rubbed her calves one at a time as if she hadn't been on her back most of the night. She wasn't wearing her pantyhose, he noticed. Where were they—purse? pocket of the white sleeveless dress?

"I called—" She leaned against the dented side of his faded black truck and swept the red hair away from her face with one big hand.

He stole a peek at her while he threw the garbage bags of scrap cloth and plastic in front of the scuffs. He had that one sticker tire must've rolled off a stack and fallen in the drainage ditch back of the Goodyear garage a year ago. He'd been saving it for another one to show up and sell as a pair, but this morning he'd decided there was no use waiting any longer.

Down the block, the first rose glow Lauralee had walked through was gone now, a tall dark figure he knew was her though he could only see a black outline till she got to the neighbor's house. That eye thing from the end over end crash. But he could still see well enough to know it was her impatient heels landing in hard clicks even as tired as she was.

The sky now spread a very pleasant yellow-orange like melted margarine, then faded onto lavender and blue-white-blue. It was the kind of sky would make a person hopeful on a Sunday morning if that person's wife hadn't been out most of the night with Cam Richards, the assistant Methodist minister at their church.

Sonny shook his head carefully like he had to so as not to shake his fretted neck bones into a headache as spectacular as that sunrise and loosen his eyesight one more notch. "What good does it do to call when you're not coming home?"

He looked at her again. Her eyes were scared, it was happening too fast. The day he'd taken their dog out to the empty field behind the house and shot it for biting the neighbor's kid, the dog's eyes had carried that same expression—halfway between saying "I didn't mean it" and "you don't either." He hadn't been able to pat the dog, offer it any comfort as it crouched on its belly, wetting the dry, hard ground in a dark spill when he put the barrel to the head and pulled the trigger. He'd closed his eyes at the last moment but imagined he heard the dog grunt like a grown man hit in the stomach the second before the explosion.

His fingers twitched on the tailgate, lifting as if to go to her of their own accord, and he stuffed them in his jeans pockets.

"I didn't mean it—" she said. "I mean, I meant, I was coming home—the whole time—" The first tear arrived and she let it roll right down her face and disappear off her chin. She had the biggest, wettest tears he'd ever seen, huge soaking things that honestly terrified him. When he'd come to in the hospital, neck broken, skull fractured, it was the puddle she was crying on the front of his hospital gown that had convinced him he was dying. It took him a while to realize he was okay. No more racing though. That about did kill him the first six months, until lately when he'd begun to feel the relief of not having to spend his weekends running flat out anymore.

When he got out of the hospital, he couldn't stay away from the tracks and had devised this patched-up thing of collecting and selling "merchandise" to race fans, garages, and drivers starting out on tiny budgets. He stared at his beat-up, grease dark hands. Wasn't much of a career, he guessed, nothing to speak of, not really. Insurance paid off their house, he'd had his old truck, and Lauralee worked at the church doing secretary stuff—well, more than that these days.

"Lauralee—" He meant to reach for her, wipe the tear away, but his eyes had distance all mixed up and he struck her instead. Not hard, but she leaned back, stunned, and avoided his other hand reaching for her. "I'm sorry—"

"You know how many times that's happened in the past year, Sonny?"

Well, now she was back to being mad. He sighed and walked over to the pile of boxes and bags he'd been loading and grabbed the cardboard stand-up of Dale Earnhardt he'd gotten from a friend at Sears Automotive in Kalamazoo a few years ago. He and cardboard Dale had split a few brews. The Dale stand-up wore his in muddy beer streaks, but Sonny figured he could get a couple of bucks out of him anyway.

"I can't help it, Lauralee."

"Never used to be this way, Sonny—" She slushed her feet through the dead grass at the curb, sending loose gravel bouncing back to the pavement.

When he closed his eyes, he could see her perfectly, bring his body in exact position to hers. He took a deep breath, the one he'd been avoiding in case the scent was on her, the familiar musk in her hair, on her arms. Though it'd been months and months since they'd—he knew he'd recognize it immediately—

She took a step toward him, and he almost said, "don't."

"You missed me, didn't you?" she murmured.

He took another breath and refused to smell the air again, but it came anyway—the damp dawn flowers, the leftover day heat of hot asphalt street, the mildew and burnt rubber from the back of the truck, and then underneath it all her musk. He closed his eyes as she came closer.

"You were all alone too long, weren't you, baby?" She reached for him, pulling his head, his permanently stiff neck against her shoulder in an awkward embrace.

Oh, he did not want to breathe now, he promised himself, but felt the dizziness like a wind starting to knock him sideways and threw his arms around her. In some mysterious act of grace, his hands caught and held on in exactly the right places. "Just for a minute—" he whispered into the full dark complex of odors caught in the hollow of her neck.

"What if I told you we were just praying?" she murmured.

"Don't," he said, trying to pull back but unable to. It was just like the times on the track when he could see there wouldn't be room to pull ahead and pass the car next to him by the corner, but he kept running side by side, three abreast sometimes, and usually the door opened—except for the last time when that new kid from Georgia had driven wheel to wheel with him. Sonny's last memory was the way the kid gave him the finger through three turns. He couldn't recall the rest. Never would, they told him.

Suddenly he pictured Lauralee on her knees praying, but he stopped himself. "I think it's gonna be a real good day, might make some real money—" He felt her body resist him, and he hurried on. "I'm taking most of that junk you hate—the scrap metal off the cars and stuff I pick up from the garage and pit areas after the big races—really, you're not gonna believe the basement or garage—"

She leaned back, her head level with his even in her bare feet. He guessed he knew where those pantyhose were. "All of it?" she asked, her eyes more suspicious than friendly.

He tried to hold her gaze, but his vision slipped off again. It was probably getting worse, he had to admit, but that was another issue. "A lot of it. An awful lot—" He gestured toward the truck.

She let go of him and turned toward the pile on the ground he was still loading. She nudged a green garbage bag with her toe. "You want my opinion, you should take this junk to the dump where it belongs, Sonny—"

He felt the old argument nosing its way back into their life. He should grow up, get a real job. Going from swap meets to race-tracks and garage sales was not a career path, she'd say.

"This is pathetic—" She bent down and picked up the half of a steering wheel from Ernie Irvin's Talladega car he'd traded a hunk of Richard Petty's Daytona bumper for. Sonny didn't tell his wife that it was the pieces from famous wrecked cars he was trying to corner the market on. Now, with her new Christian outlook, he'd probably never tell her.

"Where're your pantyhose?" He hadn't meant to say it, but because he had, now he had to stand behind the words, as stupid as they sounded. The quick fright in her face scared him too, the way she became boxed, slanted, framed doubles as his eyes worked their sick magic. Sick alright. He wanted to throw up.

"Sonny—" She stopped as the paper man drove slowly by, tossing the Sunday edition in a fat thump beside the piled boxes and bags, nodding at them before he drove on in his rusty gold '70s Buick station wagon.

"What does it take, Lauralee? I mean, what does it take anymore with you?" He picked up a small cardboard box of lug nuts, bolts, screwdrivers, wrenches, and burnt plugs, all labeled carefully from the track garages and pit areas. Earnhardt, Jarrett, Waltrip, Gordon, Elliot, Andretti, Martin, Marlin, Wallace, Musgrave, Bodine, Burton, the Labonte boys. These were his NASCAR Winston Cup favorites. He tried following Indy Cars, but it wasn't the same. He was an American boy, an American driver, meant for the heavy stock cars on American tracks. He'd tried more than once to make this point to his wife. She hadn't understood it before. No reason she'd understand what it meant for him to be selling this stuff today. Slamming the box down beside the sticker tire, he grabbed a paper bag of old driver shoes and slung it in on top of the box.

Selling? Hell, he'd give it away if he had to—he'd known that at 3 A.M. when he started packing. He'd said it again at 4 A.M. which was the last deadline for human decency he'd given her. At 5 A.M. as he pushed his few clothes into a duffel bag, dragged it to the truck, and stuffed it in the passenger side on the bench seat where the dog and his wife used to ride, he vowed to give her absolutely not one minute past 5:30. And then he'd known it for sure at 6 A.M. when he saw her long dark legs breaking the rose dawn sky, shattering it into slivers sharp enough to cut a whole new him out of what was left.

The Trouble with the Truth

I married a man who loves weddings and all I have to show for it is the gold stub of an Elvis Tour bus ticket. He'd just lost his job changing tires with the race team after he cracked a ball joint dropping the car from the jack. It fell off as the driver headed for the track. Lucky, was what they said. Could've cost us the race, maybe the car and driver too. This was the very sad story he told that night a year ago in Billy's Bar getting drunk and watching video replays of old races on the TV mounted in the corner with the sound turned off and the handicapped words printed in white across the bottom. When did they decide people need to watch TV while they drink? I asked him. We nursed our seven-and-sevens till closing time and haven't been separated since. Until now, that is. I pick up the Elvis Tour bus ticket and put it in the same box as the plastic bride and groom from the cake my cousin Mavis baked.

Five years ago Mavis went all the way to Saint Paul, Minnesota for the Vo Tech cooking course, but quit after ice sculptures and wedding cakes, her two specialties which supplement Lonnie's income as an over the road trucker. He's such a good Christian he won't take hauling jobs that don't serve the Lord, so he spends a lot of time at home watching the *700 Club* and eating pretzels in a slow, almost demented way. And drinking water. You'd think he was an Arab, Mavis complains. Mavis is also Christian and tucks little crosses into her creations, regardless of how the customer feels about it. It's become a game at receptions to find the crosses on the ice swans and sailfish, or the three tiered cakes bogged down by clumps of bright unidentifiable flowers. Mavis only got a c- on the cake section, she told me one day, but that was prejudiced on the part of the instructor who was a man. What did he know about cake baking? What Mavis is good at is texture and flavor. My own secret ingredients, she smiles whenever anyone comments. My cake was cranberry-apple flavored and the crosses sat deep inside the red and yellow clumps supposed to be roses, but resembling oranges instead. The crosses themselves were hard white sugar creations made in molds Lonnie ordered off a Christian shopping channel as a surprise when Mavis opened her business. For Easter and Christmas, Mavis makes cross cakes with three of those little sugar crosses standing in a row along the crossbeam and gives them to all her family and friends. Sometimes it feels more like a burden than a gift.

The man who loves weddings acted like Dracula when he saw the first cross cake and refused to enter the kitchen again until I hid it. He's as bad as our dog, Frank, who is so afraid of pigs that the day I brought home the big black plastic pig bank I'd won at the auto parts store where I work, he scurried out of the house and hid under the porch. I've had to hide the pig just like I hide the cross cakes when they arrive.

Maybe it's a guilty conscience, I decide after I meet his other wife Doris in Osceola a month ago. How many wives does a man need? I yell and he tells me the other one is an accident. Accident? No, a car hitting a tree is an accident, I correct him. That actually sends him out to look for a job, something no amount of nagging has been able to do. Working at the garage, he'll be able to file for divorce from his other wife and me both. We're going to get married again as soon as he's done with all the legal work, he's promised. That will give him three weddings in a row, I calculate. But there lurks in my imagination the idea that other wives could pop up, other women and weddings he's forgotten about as well.

I suppose you were drinking that time too, I ask sarcastically as we sit in the booth of the Big Chef waiting for our burgers. He gets that pig worried dog expression on his face and shrugs. He is a small, compact man, almost good at a lot of things, Doris and I have discovered. Maybe he did marry her in the accidental mood of the moment. He has a lot of those. In the garage, they can barely trust him to change the oil, patch a flat. He only keeps the job because I give them discounts on their parts at the auto store now. On our honeymoon to Graceland, he somehow broke the light fixture in the tour bus bathroom, and the rest of the way people could be heard thumping and cursing in the dark as they peed.

He started bigger in life than where he is now, that much Doris and I do know. But his story is as much a history of mistakes as weddings. Once, when he made it all the way to Busch Grand National cars, he reversed the camber on the tires at Martinsville. Instead of getting full layover on the corners, the car slid up into the wall. Well, anyone can make a mistake, he says. Doris and I know there is nothing like a man in trouble to win a woman's heart. Look at Mavis and Lonnie. Look at Jesus. Look at Doris and me.

It might be better if he took up religion, I tell Doris when we meet at Billy's Bar. Turner's garage is born again. I guess it wouldn't be the worst thing that could happen. We both stare at our rum-and-cokes with the little bubbles strung like beads up the sides of the glasses.

Doris is my height, five-five, and medium build like me. We could be cousins sooner than Mavis, who is a too tall blonde with none of the fun in her angles. We're serviceable types, Doris and me. We're the women pushing kids into cars, shoving grocery carts down aisles, working behind counters. We don't ask, how could I be so blind? Our vocabulary is limited to things like: what shall I do with the wedding photo, when do I change my driver's license, how do I tell my family? Looking at the two of us, no wonder he made a mistake, forgot he already had a wife. Like buying a second bag of flour or a book you've already read.

People forget. And he loves weddings. Desire like that can override just about anything, I guess. Doesn't necessarily make you a bad person.

Someone punches in some George Strait, who I have never particularly liked, his songs having the same qualities as his face: good-looking and bland. What we need here is some outlaw music, some Steve Earle with his junked-up drunk voice chasing the words that come stumbling along a little too fast for him. Even in the sad songs he sounds both mad and about to burst out laughing. And there's something about right now that makes me feel the same way. Doris and I heard about each other by accident from Mavis who got an order for the same cake I had at my wedding. Seems Doris's four-year anniversary is coming up and he'd fallen in love with that cranberry-apple flavor from our cake. He gave her Mavis's number. So we're meeting for the first time here.

I thought he was at the track those weekends, I say.

Doris looks at me with these blue eyes that say rain is coming down inside here, honey.

Do you think there are others? Wives, I mean.

She has been so surprised by the first second wife that I don't think her mind has traveled to that next rest stop yet. Neither of us has children. Neither of us smokes, though all around us the air is cloudy from the drinkers lighting up and blowing their exhausted day into the dark room. Billy's has knotty pine walls so old the varnish is orange and a brown linoleum floor so dotted with black cigarette burns it looks like the original pattern. Set off the road, there's a sprawl of gravel parking lot in front so everyone can see who's here. I personally know four or five different guys who park their pickups at the used car lot a block away and walk over so their wives don't find them here. It's late afternoon, and outside the sun is shining like some holy war is about to begin, and the way it stabs through the holes where the black paint has peeled off the front windows, you'd think it was the Almighty Himself pointing fingers at all of us crouched down in dark safety here. I try to imagine the cake Doris orders showing up tiered with crosses marching to the top like tiny soldiers. Scare the bejesus out of him.

You remember that time he worked as the gas man at Watkins Glen? Doris stops and takes a drink.

I nod. That wasn't his fault either. They told him to get every drop in and it splashed back into his eyes.

She looks at the table, brushes the scarred green formica with her hand, then looks at the jukebox. Wonder who he married that time?

There is this instant picture of the race at Daytona where he lost the thread chaser and they couldn't fix the stud while the other cars raced around and around like sonic zippers. I drain my rum-and-coke and raise two fingers. We're both going to need more.

I guess we should be mad or something. But I'm not pissed off. Not at you, anyway. I guess I'm not mad at him either. What do you suppose that means?

She shrugs and finishes her drink, using the tip of her tongue to lick the ice cubes clean. I'd done that same thing a moment before. When you get down to it we're all pretty much alike, it seems, and that makes the hair thin differences important. Maybe that's what he notices, and while it looks like what he's doing is buying the same shirt over and over, what he's really doing is falling in love with these tiny differences. I could probably pick us out of any crowd, we'd be so alike, but he'd know the truth, how each of us has come to stand in the sorrow of time.

So Doris and I sit here a while longer, watching the sun go down through the holes in the painted window, the fingers of light slowly pulling back until all that is left is spread on the gravel parking lot—pink, then gray, then the yellow green of the fluorescents coming on. On the jukebox a CD sticks, making a snap snap like a bug zapper for half an hour before someone notices. Doris and I watch the endless negotiations of the men and women at the surrounding tables and the bar. After a few more drinks, they begin to remind me of cars racing around a track, bumping and pushing, running close enough side by side they could carry on a conversation if not for the roaring engines. There is so much noise here tonight, Doris and I have to repeat each word in a shout and find our sentences getting shorter and shorter until finally we only gesture and nod. We get grace this way, for a few minutes, the perfect understanding that can come briefly when two people are drawn and held with enough force to a single place. I figure the man who loves weddings must recognize how irresistable we all seem to each other at moments like this, just before our world dissolves again with another crashing disaster. He never says mistakes were made. He calls them accidents, and it's hard to hate a man like that. That's the trouble with the truth.

Jonis Agee

Losing Downforce

He felt his car wash up the track again, the tires going away some more. Louise was the first woman crew chief he'd ever had, and he was so bound and determined to have his say, he'd made the mistake of not taking on new tires last pit stop. He fought the front end, then the back wobbling toward the wall, and inched back down to the groove the other cars were driving in.

Jimmie appeared in his side mirror trying to nudge on by. Jimmie was the leader and if he lapped him, he'd have to work that much harder to get back, so he moved down, running side by side toward the corner. "Shit, oh shit," he muttered to the silence of the radio. Louise wasn't reassuring him the way she should be. Damn women. He felt the car slow with Jimmie tucked right up next to him, close enough to french kiss.

"Jimmie's on your left side trying to get by," the spotter crackled over the radio so loudly it made his ears ring even with the roar of engine and track noise numbing his head. "No shit, Sherlock." He fought the wheel, glancing over at the flash of black he caught on the right. Perfect, Lane's black car was inching up trying to pass high where he'd been running all day, to capture the lead from Jimmie. He could feel the car really starting to go away, the aerodynamics messed up with the side-by-side racing.

"Better get outta there," the spotter said as the corner loomed ahead.

"Come on, come on," he urged, but the car didn't have anything more to give him. Jimmie's nose edged in front and Lane was coming down on him.

"Watch it—"

Jimmie's bump sent the car shivering in front. Shit—he wasn't going to make the corner as he nudged up toward Lane who tried to get out of the way and couldn't when the rear end let go and they both ploughed right up the track into the wall, once, then spun, then down and around, hit again by another car, then into the inside barrier, hit again, spinning until the sheared metal came to a shattered stop nosing the concrete.

"You okay? You okay?" the radio kept squawking, but he was too pissed to answer. He ripped the net off the window and started to climb out into the arms yanking at him. He was going to kick the shit out of that Lane kid, then get Jimmie after the race. The arms kept arguing with him as he struggled toward the other car smoking a few yards away.

Later, when he'd been released by the medical team and driven back to the garage, Louise just looked at him and shook her head. "Perfectly good car," was all she said.

"It had a push," he insisted.

She eyed him in a way that reminded him of a lot of women he'd lied to—his mom, his teachers, and lately his wife. What the hell gave women the right to know when a man wasn't telling the truth? Another man would give him that, know he was lying, but give it to him for the excuse he needed. A person needed some pride.

"You could've won that race," she said. "The setup was perfect. Best it's run all season." She was his age, early forties, and looking at her jaw was like looking in the mirror when he shaved. The thing that irritated him most was that the dark roots of her blonde hair always showed. Like she didn't think it worth the bother. His wife always looked nice. She made it a practice now that the television people were around all the time. With the gimme cap on, Louise's hair sticking out the sides, you couldn't see the roots, but in the garage you could and it bothered him.

"She's the best we can get and lucky to have her," the team owner had told him. "She's taken Carl's team to the top five year ends in the Busch Lights ten times. Now you need to settle down and drive, let us worry about the rest." But it worried him. First the old crew chief's let go, now a woman. Next thing, they'd be looking for a new driver.

He waited while she consulted the printouts on the race, running the columns of numbers with that short, thick, no-nonsense finger of hers. Suddenly, he wished she smoked. Something. His wife had told him not to cause trouble, they needed the job to finish putting the kids through college. They'd been a young, hot couple in bed, popping out the five kids one-two-three like marbles on a plate, racing featherlites and outlaws on dirt tracks, running from one place to another in their camper. Those were good, crazy times, not like today. Hell, they used to duct tape the cars together to keep 'em going, and they listened to him, did what he said because he was the driver and trying to win, and he did, that was how he got to Winston Cup and was Rookie of the Year, and then won a race or two a season. Now he was down to praying for a top twenty finish. They were going to dump him. He could feel it. This Louise, she was the beginning of the end.

"Probably my fault the tires went away right after the pit," he offered, willing to concede a little.

"Uh huh," she grunted and turned over a sheet. The skin at her throat was crepey too. Freckled and angry looking from all the days at the tracks in the hot sun. What made a woman want to give up her beauty like that?

"We were running so good, I wanted to get the bonus points for leading a few laps, put in a strong top ten finish. That's why I asked for the short pit. Car was really hooked up there for a while," he tried, "you all did a good job."

She put the sheets down on the shiny hood of the backup car. "Think the car had a push coming into turn two?" Those faded blue-white eyes stared right back at him, trying to get something out of him. He'd as soon talk to the clothes on the line as her right now. Her eyes about the color of his favorite pair of jeans, the holey ones he'd brought with him from the dirt track days, couldn't get one leg in 'em now. There were months when they were all he had to put on and he wanted to remember that. Once he caught his wife dressing the Halloween scarecrow on the front yard in those jeans and he'd thrown a regular fit. Where'd a person get eyes the color of old Levis anyway?

He shrugged.

"What do you think—broken shock mount, maybe?" She tilted her head at him in a way he couldn't imagine any man finding endearing. Not that she was bad-looking, she was okay. She was just, well, truth be told, he never liked any of his crew chiefs, not really.

He shrugged again.

"Set of bad tires then?" She gestured toward the heap of metal behind her. "Hard to say now."

He felt something in him let go. Okay, okay, have it your own way, he heard a voice sigh. His chest got smaller and he almost hoped it was some kind of injury so she'd feel a little sorry, but he'd checked out fine. Couple of bruises coming on his legs and arms, but nothing. He was damn lucky. Did she know how lucky it was out there today? He might have been killed—

"Doc says you're fine. Too shaken up to do a few test runs on the backup car after the race?" She looked him over like one of her damn cars, biting the edge of her lower lip in a callused spot that looked red and chapped. "We get the setup right, we can use it next time. And we can check for that push—"

"I should've listened." He couldn't say, "to you."

She picked up the telemetry sheets and started to roll them in a thick circle, her knuckles red and weathered-looking.

"The tires went away. Then Jimmie tapped me and that was all she wrote." He felt his face flush and burn as she looked out the big open doors of the garage toward the roar and whine of the cars on the track followed by the wake of crowd noise that came as an after echo of each lap.

"We're not getting any younger, you and me." She looked back at him with a slight curve of smile on her lips which surprised him. "Can't afford disorganized thinking."

"No," he admitted.

"Well, an old dog can still hunt. Just needs a few more tricks to keep up. Think about it." She pulled her hat off, and he could see the lines on her forehead, the commas beside her mouth, and the patchy net on her cheeks. "We're bringing up that kid from the truck circuit next season. Running two cars. You can help."

There it was. Maybe better to kiss the wall goodnight. He pictured the final slamming force, the fiery flip in the air, the magnificent fireball tumble down the track, the collapsing chest, windpipe, face. No—he still had kids to put through college, the mortgage to finish paying off on their house in Holcomb so his wife could be comfortable. Insurance wouldn't cover all that. What would she do then? She was his age, five kids out of that body had taken its toll, too. He tried to picture her working like Louise. No, she'd worked her last day, he'd told her when he finally started making some money. The day he signed with the team, he'd picked her up at the supper club where she tended bar and given her the keys to a new car.

That was the dream, not this other thing, the stubborn I'm-right-about-it-all thing he'd been racing on lately. Like some dirt track kid, full of attitude, not caring how many times you wrecked 'cause you always walked away. Those days were going away now too. There was the bad crash at Talladega three years ago, another at Rockingham nine months later when he'd finally come back from his injuries. Darlington was lucky, and today—

"I was lucky today," he said softly, looking out at the bright blur of cars.

"That you were, my friend," she put a hand on his shoulder. "But I have a feeling things can get real interesting—once you stop running off your balls and let your brains do some work for a change."

He laughed. "Maybe a combination?"

"I'll leave that ratio up to you," she said. "By the way, Lane's been medivacked and Jimmie's engine let go while you were being checked over."

"Hell of a day." He looked around the garage at the tools strewn everywhere, half-empty cans of pop sitting on every flat surface, and the racecars resting bright and hopeful as young tropical birds on their racks.

You Know I Am Lying

As my mother says, cattle have a good life, but they pay for it in the end. But then, she was always at sixes and sevens. What does that mean? I used to ask her, but she'd go on pulling the cucumbers off the vines with that little tug and twist and placing them careful as eggs in the basket she carried. I don't see those anymore, the rectangular farm baskets that fit over your arm with the deep sides. Not an Easter basket kind of affair. The slats were wide and sturdy enough to carry quart jars of stewed tomatoes or pickles. Out in the garden with the long rows separating the vegetables, she'd remind me not to plant the cukes near the cantaloupe if I wanted to keep their flavors apart.

All summer, I'd watch the cuke and squash and melon vines to make sure they stayed segregated to their own sections along the fence bordering the cattle pen so it was only a short throw in the winter tossing the manure over the fence to make the soil rich and worm-thick in the spring. My job was hoeing and it is a job I hope never to repeat now that so much has changed. I will miss those pickles though. I still have the Heinz pickle pin Mom's great-grandma got as a child at the first World's Fair in Chicago in 1893. Not many people knew about the exhibit, but I come from a long line of avid picklers and it was in the genes to track down that booth and come home with the prized pin that's been handed down with the family Bible through the women until Mom had only me, and that meant a male getting possession of things he shouldn't, I guess. Mr. Heinz was a man, I reassure myself. He thought up the card enticing fairgoers to his booth for a free gift —the pin. It was that one brush with fame—Mr. Heinz himself handing my great-grandmother the pickle pin she wore first as a brooch and later on a thin gold chain like a locket—that remains our family story. Until now that is.

The auctioneer has packed his truck and left. The yard is cluttered with flyers, paper napkins from the food table, and pop cans, and inside the house here, well, each room has one little thing left over to remind me—things nobody wanted. The half barn door we used as a coffee table after Dad and Uncle Harry had the argument arm-wrestling. As a baldheaded man said when I told him the price, "For seven bucks, I could buy me some chickens." I know, it still looks exactly like what it was: the barn stall door Mom had me lift off its hinges and haul to the house. The manure stains are so deep, no amount of scrubbing could pull them out of the wood. Kneeling, I run my hand over the edge worn smooth and shiny brown by years of hands pushing and pulling it. My father's and his father's and his father's hands, and then last of all mine. Maybe it was taking the door down, bringing it in the house that made things begin to fail in general, like Mom used to hint. I've wondered about that.

Hoeing the garden meant chasing the bull snakes that liked to sun themselves in the hot dirt waiting for mice and toads and small rabbits. They were never in a good mood, but then neither was I, out there in the heat of the day, my shirt tossed over the chicken wire fence, jeans sticking to the backs of my legs, my skin pringly tight with sun baking itself into me. And my hands, no matter if I wore gloves or not, my hands would blister before they callused. Adding more to the history of that damn hoe than I ever wanted, I think I wore that handle smooth in the years I spent out there. Now some woman took it home to paint it red and use it for her rose garden. She probably only has to deal with garter snakes and they're quick to get out of your way.

Bull snakes, they'll bite, you bother them. It hurts like getting stung by a handful of bees. And the way they lie there, so big and thick, like rattlers, every time I came on one of those critters I had to remind myself we didn't have poisonous snakes here in Iowa. They'd rear up and open their jaws and act mad as all get out, trying to convince me I didn't need to hoe out that ragweed with such a good start in the bean patch. It was all I could do not to bring that sharp edge down on their heads, but Mom thought it bad luck and worse to kill a snake in the garden. I'd of liked her to get out there and have to chop weeds around those pissy old men. That's what I decided one day, they were lying around like they were retired old farmers, my grandfather up to the house those couple of years before he died. They probably had all kinds of youngsters out there working themselves to death too.

Dad was on that tractor from dawn till dark a lot of days. Seems like we were always haying or getting ready to hay. He'd go to town and hire some day workers, bring 'em out and we'd work like sons of bitches until noon, the hired men doing half of what I could do since they weren't used to the heat and pure drudgery of lifting bale after bale and throwing it on the wagon and then having to stack them in the barn when the wagon got full. They got a taste of what I did and you could tell how grateful they were for the day money as they piled into the truck for the ride back to town at dark, despite the good food Mom fixed and the jar of pickles she sent home with each of them. I tried to tell her these men were not going to want those pickles, but she thought it was my usual selfish nature and ignored me. But I'll tell you, about the saddest thing a person could see is finding the sweet pickles you have helped your own mother make swimming in broken glass down the end of the road in the deep weeds by the mailbox.

After she filled the basket with cukes, she'd bring them in and dump them in the sink, and for some reason, there was always some stupid grasshopper trying to spring out but sliding down the slick porcelain sides instead. It was my job to catch it and throw it back outside, though why in the world we would be adding grasshoppers to the world, I couldn't say. It was like the snake deal though, you weren't allowed to kill bugs while she was making her pickles. Pickle day wasn't quite like other canning days. Grapes she harvested late summer, making thick sweet juice and jelly when the mood struck her of a morning before it got hot. Jellies got made all the time, in fact. Tomatoes were a nasty time, taking all day for days, the steam boiling up in clouds that coated the cabinets with sweat that dripped back down in brown streaks, and my mother's face and hands looking scalded themselves as she slipped the skins off the tomatoes, hot from the water, and pushed the red flesh whole into jars or smashed them into the sieve for the juice. Her hands would be raw looking until well into October from canning, and I'd shy from her touch on my cheek which I see now was not the right thing to do.

Pickle days she'd hum to herself as she took the clean cukes wrapped in a clean dishtowel she made from flour sacks and went down to the basement, leaving me standing at the top of the stairs to turn off the light when she had landed safely. She was ever an economical person. And particularly guarded about those pickles. No man in our family had ever had the recipe and she wasn't about to share it with me. Being her only child, I used to wonder, but didn't dare raise the issue. So each summer she would make her pickles, enter them in the county and state fairs, and always win a prize. I'm making it sound a lot easier than it was. Sometimes in the middle of the night, I'd hear her creeping down those stairs to check her pickles, muttering to herself and banging around in the kitchen if things weren't going right, or humming back up to bed if they were fine. I should've known how important they were to her. I mean, it doesn't take a genius to see that.

I go into the kitchen to see what's left. One can of Miller and a rumpled piece of old lettuce on the counter next to where the fridge stood. There's a black square of dirt, dust, and insect bodies in its place, and I drop the lettuce in the middle like topping because that's about what this feels like: a dirt sandwich. I pop the beer and take a quick swig, swallowing before I can really taste the warm grainy suds. Outside, the sun is dropping back behind the hay barn, hanging a moment there like a red-orange balloon caught in the trees of the windbreak on the hill at the edge of the eighty-acre pasture. There was a time when I studied the sky. As a boy growing up alone on a small southern Iowa farm, I had to invent a lot when I wasn't working. About this time in August, for instance, Venus is very low and brilliant in the sky after sunset. Then gradually you'll find Spica and Mars left of it. Procyon in Canis Minor, the little dog, will be the brightest star in the constellation. The heads of Castor and Pollux, the Gemini twins, will be to the moon's left. And reddish Betelgeuse, the shoulder of Orion, with Procyon and Sirius form the nearly equilateral Winter Triangle. When I made that discovery, it was as if winter was always out there, all the time, just waiting for its turn. The year got a lot shorter after that.

I salute the sun's last red lip at the horizon with the can of warm beer and put it down. Around me the house ticks and creaks as if it's restless now that the floors and walls are freed of our clutter. One of my mother's old dishtowels sits wadded up on the counter which looks dirty for the first time that I can remember. Automatically, I swipe at the black dots of bug carcasses and crumbs and sweep them into the sink, turning on the water to wash them away. There is a big mauve stain in the middle of the towel when I flap it open and shake it. Straining wild plum pulp for jelly. That summer Dad offered to pay me a nickel a sparrow to clear the thicket so there'd be enough plums for her jelly. But he told me not to mention it to her. Every morning she'd ask me what I was doing down there when I came back to the house scratched and sweaty, my hands dotted with blood. I'd lie and smile mysteriously, counting the profit silently. After the first day, I negotiated the deal to include the eggs whose smashed shells I would present for verification along with the dead bodies. Sparrows were a nuisance around the farm, dirtying the grain, eating fruit and vegetables intended for us, and creating such a clatter, it drove my father wild.

After the first couple of days it seemed like a simple job. I dug out the catalog Dad got from something called "U.S. Cavalry, World's Finest Military and Adventure Equipment" to prepare my assault, and marked several items that might be useful in addition to my BB gun. What I wanted was a knife, something to lop the sparrow heads off so I wouldn't be stuck with the whole body which ended up stinking and sometimes maggoty by the end of the hot day when my dad would come out to the tool shed with me to make the count. The Seal Team Knife was over a hundred dollars, but it was at the top of my list. I'd settle for the World War II Commemorative Knife, which I thought my dad would like since he'd been there, but I put the German-style Paratrooper Knife with the side saw-edge for versatility at $12.99 as a realistic choice. And I needed a scope and a mount. The 4 × 25 Assault was waterproof and fogproof which would allow me to kill in the rain too. Checking the prices though, I knew my chances of getting either were pretty slim unless I saved for them myself. Which I could do if I made enough off these sparrows. Then with the scope, I could make even more and save for something else.

By the end of the first week, the sparrows were so suspicious of me that they raised a panicked cry and flew frantically in and out and over the thicket every time I appeared. Since I'd raided all the nests within reach, I faced the problem of climbing the thorny trees for those higher up with the sparrows now dive-bombing me the way they did crows and hawks in their territory. It hurt, too. Those tiny sharp-pointed beaks left dots of blood that dried to sore scabs on my scalp which I didn't dare show my mother. Then there were the eggs. At first it was fun throwing them as hard as I could on the ground or heaving them at the steers when they pushed up to feed. It always seemed so hilarious to watch the expression on their dumb white faces when the egg popped open on their heads and dripped down. I liked getting paid every day too. Then one afternoon I noticed something. Some of the eggs were going to hatch, and instead of a nice clean little yolk, there was this pink wet thing dripping bloody yellow. Instead of lifting my foot to squash it, I turned away, keeping track of these things out of the corner of my eye. By the next morning some of them were gone, slurped up by the barn cats or raccoons or snakes, but one was still there, the form in motion as if it were trying to wriggle back into life, until I leaned close enough to see the insects and maggots replacing it.

My father called me lazy when I told him most of the sparrows were gone and the rest were too smart now. My mother was shelling peas every morning to be put in the pressure cooker before they were canned that week. One morning while I sat with her, trying to keep up with her quick fingers, she nodded toward the gun in the corner and said, "I know what you were doing out there." I felt as if I'd thrown a jar of her precious pickles in the ditch myself.

It was a bumper plum crop my father and I harvested in twenty-gallon buckets. My mother made the jelly dutifully, but not very joyfully while my father helped. He was his usual laughing self, drinking beer and kidding around. That towel though, I remember how she took a brand new one she'd just made to strain the pulp because it kept clogging the wire sieve, and how the strands of pulp had that red-blue cast that looked so like old rotting muscles and nerves, and how my father dragged two fingers through it and leaned his head back and dropped that mess in his mouth and somehow that reminded me of the sparrows. I have no stomach for plums anymore.

My father's troubles came later, from the stomach problems he'd been having since the war. Short-gut syndrome, they called it. His intestine was partially destroyed by the time I was well into high school, and they were trying to figure out if he needed a new liver too. The VA wasn't particularly helpful until they heard about a study being conducted with experimental drugs for transplants that would be paid for by the drug company. Well, that was not such a good thing, as it turned out.

With my boyhood military career cut short, I took a brief run at raising steers for 4-H, but my heart wasn't in four-leggeds. I still worked haying and hoeing and painting and cutting weeds and grass and helping Mom, but I didn't feel as connected to the farm. One day I was poking around back of the old hog barn when I found a car chassis. The sheet metal body had long since been dismantled piece by piece for repairing the hog fence and barn roof which was tin. I knew this because Dad and I had put in the replacements. Hooking up the small Ford tractor, I pulled the chassis free and hauled it up to rest near the tool shed where I began to work on something I could ride around in after the cows or over the fields when I had to take lemonade to dad. Those were my selfless plans in the beginning. I think my mom was happy to see me spending my time on construction rather than destruction, and she was busy making pickles anyway. I salvaged a motor off the abandoned Allis-Chalmers that could still hump along like a spider on a mirror if you babied it, but lacked the strength for real work. It was the first motor I took apart and got back together with most of the pieces in the right places. Just puttering around the barnyard, maneuvering around the chicken coop and cistern back up between the mulberry trees—what a proud day. I'd cut the chassis down and rewelded it. I'd known enough to do that since I was eight. For safety, I had to know how to help Dad if anything went wrong. I learned to drive early and could go anywhere, even the highway down to the hay and cornfields, on the tractor.

I was so thrilled that first week, I left the hose running in the garden and flooded the cukes so bad several vines washed out and I had to kneel there with my knees and toes sinking in the mud trying to rebuild the mounds before Mom came out and saw the destruction. The next day when the mud baked dry, it looked like I'd been trying to leave casts of my hands and feet all over her cuke bed. She only looked heartbroken and didn't say anything when she saw it.

That wasn't the worse thing I did, I think now, as the yard turns violet with evening and the barn swallows stab in and out of the dark entrance feeding. From somewhere east, a swoop of bats comes in that too quick way that says they're not birds, flying flawlessly between wires, trees, barns, and sheds, to disappear across the field.

By high school I was building and modifying engines and cars for other kids who wanted to show off or go racing around. I wasn't home much, or rather I was here, but I was out in the shed where I worked, having reclaimed it from the debris of three generations of farmers, pouring a good concrete floor myself and hooking up the wiring despite Dad's predictions that I was going to burn the whole place down. Thinking back on it, I didn't hoe much anymore, didn't pick vegetables either. I guess Mom was on her own the way I was. I never gave it much thought. That's the way kids are, the volume in your own world turns up so loud you can't see or hear anybody else. Then when I had one semester to go, a call came from Mom's cousin Albert down in North Carolina asking if I would be interested in coming to work for him. I'd written him a few times after she told me who he was, and he'd never answered, but I never gave up. I just couldn't. Albert built racecars and said he had an opening, one of the guys up and quit on him. I wasn't going to get rich, but I'd learn a heck of a lot.

Mom and Dad were both against it, Dad partly because he was worried about Mom since he was so weak with diarrhea and dehydration from the intestinal failure. He'd lost a lot of weight and took a lot longer to get chores done, but he still wouldn't let me do much. He'd put the fields in the soil bank and hadn't planted for three years so by the time the offer came up our fields were filled with weeds we'd turn over for green manure each fall. He'd given up all but a couple of steers for beef and a single hog to butcher in the fall, which was like killing a family member. Mom told me not to worry, but said I couldn't leave until I graduated high school. Two nights later I left, driving the Chevy with the rebuilt motor that was barely legal in anybody's book in

Iowa. I was hoping those southerners would be more tolerant of loud engines and speed.

I haven't been a bad son. My parents were just a little old-fashioned. When they tried the transplant, Dad lingered for a while, always on the verge of rejection until the infection swept in and took him away. Mom, well, her heart was weak, it turns out. She didn't last the winter, living out here with her sister. I came back some, when I could, in between races, and then a bit longer in winter these past three years. It wasn't until I was getting ready for the sale here, two days ago, when I went to the basement to drag stuff upstairs, that I realized what had happened.

See, I'd avoided the fruit cellar, as we called the little room lined with floor-to-ceiling pine plank shelves for canned fruit and vegetables. I'd already hauled the big, thick, gray sauerkraut tub up-stairs, the old iron bedstead I slept in once I started high school, all the grease stiff Carhartts and caps and moth eaten wool coats and rotting rubber boots, and the mangle Mom used to iron the sheets and pillowcases so they were smooth and perfect, which was a bastard to wrangle up those stairs with the turn at the landing. The last thing left to do down there was the fruit cellar, so I went up and got a cold beer and a flashlight and went back down. I'd never liked that room as a kid, dreaded opening the door on the quick scurry and the air like a breath just let out and about to be taken in again. Although we set mousetraps, there would always be mice in there, trying to figure a way through glass and metal. They were fatally optimistic. There were huge spiders too, with nests I'd have to break apart to retrieve whatever Mom wanted for dinner. Seemed like she never sent me there in the morning—no, it was always late afternoon, I remember, early evening in winter when the sun was set and the basement was that too quiet dark. Even later, when I began to sleep down there, I avoided the fruit cellar if I could. Usually I was too tired from school and farm work and work on the cars to do anything but fall straight across the bed into a dead sleep by then. Now I opened the door, giving the room plenty of advance notice, saying, "Okay, alright, here I come—" as I pulled the light cord to the burned-out bulb and had to turn on the flashlight to sweep along the shelves.

I guess I expected the shelves to be full from last summer's crop. Instead the boards were empty except for dust and a couple of sprung mousetraps with the mouse so long dead it was flat and brittle as old paper when I shoved at it with the flashlight. Even the spiders had abandoned the place, their torn webs hanging in gray dusty strands below which were the anonymous bits of insect pieces. Then I noticed up on the top shelf a row of jars which required a ladder to reach. I had to go back upstairs to bring down the stepladder and replace the burned-out bulb before I could examine the jars closely.

Each jar was filled with pickles, whose oblong bodies rested like deformed fetuses in the cloudy liquid, with a label stating as always the type and the year and the award they had won. Jars for every year I could remember, in precise order, which came abruptly to an end two years before I left for Albert's. I turned the flashlight on and examined the pine board, brushing the dust away, hoping for the ring that would say the missing jars had once rested there. Then I rechecked the other dates, squinting there in the twilight of the sixty-watt bulb. It was true, of course, she'd stopped and I hadn't even noticed. Hell, I hadn't noticed she wasn't serving them at meals either. I probably couldn't tell you what meals I'd had with my parents those last few years. In fact, I'd be lying if I said I thought about anything but myself during the past six years. I'd come home and see how thin and frail Dad was, how tired Mom was, but I couldn't, you see, I just couldn't come back here and take up where I left off the day I found that chassis.

I look around the kitchen one last time, trying to memorize the stained sink, where the stove and refrigerator and table and chairs stood, the cabinets, and the view out the window which looks right at the shed I spent all those nights in. She must have stood here like I am now, watching the yard light come on, the barn cats tiptoe out into the pasture, my form bent over the engine concentrating so completely on my betrayal.

So here I am, the proud possessor of a Heinz pickle pin and the check from a farm we'd been able to keep in our family for three generations. Not much of a check at that, not anywhere near enough. You know I'd be lying if I said that it was.

Getting the Heat Up

"Colly's just had another close encounter of the concrete kind," the announcer said in a tired voice, "but he's alright
folks. He's moving around in there, now the net's down and he's
waving."

Marbeth bit her lower lip and shook her head as Colly climbed
out of the window of the car and whirled to face the oncoming
cars. When he spotted the black and orange forty-six, he shook
his fist and had to be held back by the trackmen getting ready to
drag the car out of the way. She turned and started back for the
garage area so she could help pack up their gear. Same thing all
summer. He'd run some good laps and then skate around like
Dorothy Hamill.

Benny was already shoving tools into the dresser-sized chest,
and his red face told it all. He wasn't going to be wasting any
more of his nights and weekends following them around. "I tole
him about getting off that corner!" Benny waved a wrench at her,
then slammed it into the gaping drawer so hard a screwdriver
bounced out. When he bent to pick it up, his belly bagged down
to his knees and blocked the cement floor so he had to grope for
the tool at his feet. His face was even redder when he straightened, panting, the front of his T-shirt splotched with sweat. Unlike the other mechanics, Benny was almost always clean, down
to his small pink fingers with the child-soft nails he trimmed

with a quick clip of his front teeth. Marbeth secretly watched him do it and wondered.

She leaned against the doorway as he slammed more tools around. It was the same thing every race. Colly wrecked the car and Benny punished the tools. Although he was careful with the tire pyrometer he'd picked up from Mark Martin's crew that time at Watkins Glen, she noticed. And the rubber wedges for the springs. He always counted those carefully and kept them in their own section in the second to bottom drawer. When he bent with his back toward her, she didn't get the customary view of a fat butt. Benny managed to buy trousers that fit and a belt to hold them up. She couldn't figure it out. Even Colly, as skinny as he was, ended up with his rear end in her face half the time. He wouldn't wear a belt though. Nor underwear. At first she'd thought that was sexy, or at least endearing. Now, well, now—

"Benny—" she began.

He picked up the bungee cords and blue and black rolls of tape they used to hold the car together on nights when Colly took longer to wreck it. Running the cords through the tape rolls, he hooked them together and held them up. "It isn't even about engines anymore, Marbeth. He's got all the speed in the world, I seen to that. Me and Ray, we worked like dogs." He shook the bundle in his hands at her. "This is what it comes down to. And that's not right. You can't tell me that's right." He put it in the drawer next to the spring rubbers, and she saw a small slice of dirt on the shoulder of his pale yellow t-shirt. It was all she could do not to go over there and brush at it. She stuck her hands in her back pockets so she wouldn't move.

"I know, honey," she crooned as he pushed his hand through his dark brown hair he kept short on the sides and long on top so it flopped over his eyes and parted for his big nose like a sheepdog. Usually he wore the hat she'd given the crew Christmas before last, with Colly's grandfather's hardware and grocery logo on it: Four Way Store. Their only sponsor. Everybody else looked at them like they were crazy when they asked for support. Most people on the midwestern circuit said Colly was on a borrowed string of bad luck and didn't have any to call his own. And last night the old gentleman had finally passed. There was a kind of mean triumph in his father's eyes when he looked at Colly at the breakfast table. They hadn't spoken for months over the bitterness of family money being poured into racing.

"He's gonna say we missed the setup." Benny flopped his arms like a big flightless bird. "Or something about the goddamned tires. Not enough heat in 'em, needed stickers, needed scuffs, and on and on and on."

Over the steady engine roar on the track they could hear the howling crowd heaving up and down in great waves that washed over the stands and broke up in the garages which were really stalls in a three-sided pole barn set back in a cornfield. The hot green creaking scent mingled with the exhaust and oil of the cars that afternoon as she'd stood behind the garage while they worked on the car. She'd watched the silver-tassled tops in the valley and hills beyond blow, glistening in the sun like waves on a lake with that odd life under the surface look water always had. In the distance a field of soybeans seemed as flat and luxurious as deep green velvet, the real kind like her Aunt Marye's throw pillows, and the dark corn glittered like satin rivulets valleying down to the bottomland. That was where she focused in the hot July wind, not the great mound of junked cars caught between the pole barn garages and the old dairy barn shedding brittle white paint in finger sized strips, half-shielded by a line of straight, mournful Lombardy poplars. Over the past seven years, Heison had gradually leased out all the crop land and given himself like an unwilling lover to car racing. The bank had made it clear that cars made money, not cows, he told people, and after that he kept the dirt track clean as new concrete with the big air-conditioned John Deere tractor he'd managed to save when the rest of his farm went belly-up. His wife still kept chickens, and during the hot afternoons they'd come pecking for food along the edges of the barns and under the stands, then squat down and hollow out a cool place in the dusty shade for a quick doze. When the wind was right, there'd be that feathers-and-ammonia smell of the chicken house cutting sharp as acid across the tongue.

"Maybe the Earl May Garden Center in Oskaloosa will come on board like Colly thinks." She reached for the empty Coke can lying near her. Heison had rules about leaving things clean the way you found them.

"Here—" Benny reached out for the can and she had to take three steps to hand it to him so he could arc it over her head into the trash barrel behind her. When it rattled down inside, he smiled and she saw those pale blue eyes shine something sexy. Not like the moment before when they were flat as china plates and reminded her of the wall-eyed pinto she used to ride on her uncle Darwin's farm. The no-good horse that bit her on the top of her head when she wasn't looking. She'd fixed him though, punched him a good one in the nose. He'd jerked the lead rope out of her hand and galloped back down the hundred-acre pasture, scattering cows every which way, but after that, he'd been more careful with his teeth.

She was standing close enough to smell the green pear sweat and see the dark hair on Benny's arms beaded with tiny drops. He sighed, and the big barrel chest and belly rose and fell like an animal of its own trapped inside the pale yellow tee with the Four Way logo she'd had made for the team—the best she could do for uniforms. Benny's still looked good as new. Colly's was almost worn out, like he'd used it to strain the oil or something.

"He's a liar-dog, Marbeth. Earl May wouldn't give Colly a cardboard box. Now his granddaddy's gone, he'll be lucky his daddy don't kick you all out." Benny started to put a hand on her shoulder, and she felt her body edge toward it, but he stopped and brushed the front of his shirt as if the little smear of dirt were there instead of behind him where he couldn't see.

"It's not all his fault, Benny." Here she was, she couldn't stop herself, it was such an old reflex. "Maybe the gear ratio was wrong."

Benny grabbed her shoulders, both of them, and dug his fingers in. "Look at me, Marbeth, look!"

She tried to pull back but he hung on and pulled her toward him instead until she found herself staring up into those window-blue eyes lit with anger. He was a lot bigger and taller than she was. "It wasn't wedge or gear ratio or downforce. He wasn't tight or loose. He didn't flat-spot. The tires were fine, they weren't too cold, they had enough heat in them, they've always been fine. The truth is, Colly can't drive for shit. He's a shitty driver. He's lucky he hasn't killed someone out there. Lucky he's not dead himself. He's living in a dream world, Marbeth. ESPN fantasy time. Best thing his grandpa ever did for him was die. Probably saved Colly's life—yours too maybe."

She twisted and he let her go. "And if he doesn't keep racing, he'll probably die then too, Benny."

She tried to stare him down, but couldn't, and he shook his head and turned toward the stack of tires. He lifted the top tire off a set of scuffs and let it down carefully so it wouldn't pick up any loose screws or debris. Rolling it past her, he said, "I quit."

"Can't you wait till he—" She looked around frantically. There had to be something to say or do here. She heard the thump as he lifted the tire onto the bed of the pickup outside.

When he came back, she tried to lift the next tire for him, but he took it in his arms like a platter. "Let me do it." He tipped the tire and let it down. It swerved and ran over her foot before he could balance it. "Shoot—I'm sorry," —He held the tire steady with the fingertips of one hand and touched her arm with the other. "You alright?"

She brushed at his fingers and nodded. "You never let me do anything."

He licked his lips, started to say something, then shook his head and pushed the tire forward. She stuck her foot out and spilled it over on its side. Then she kicked it, kicked it again and again as hard as she could. Benny just stood there, arms folded, until she stopped, her toes aching in her sneaker.

"Those aren't cheap, you know," he grinned.

"Doesn't matter anymore, does it?"

"Think he'll quit?"

"Quit? Oh Christ, Benny, he thinks he's going to Winston Cup in a couple of years."

"Has to finish a few races before that's gonna happen. He should take up demolition derby or something." He gave the tire a loud whomp with the toe of his shoe. "The way he wrecks cars, maybe he was born to be a body man."

She laughed.

"How come you women always go for the drivers?"

"How come you never tried driving?"

He turned his hands over and inspected the palms smudged from the tires. "You know I was watching this crocodile show the other night on cable? They said a warmer nest produces more males and a cooler nest will give you more females. Just the way of it, I guess. I'm good with these hands—" He held out his large palms with the small, almost finicky fingers.

"But you don't know, not for sure, do you?" She measured her palms against his so their fingertips rested against each other's wrists and she thought she could feel the blood begin to pulse simultaneously in their blue-sheathed veins.

He flipped his hands and grabbed her wrists. "And you could be another Tammy Jo Kirk, but I don't see you out there."

As the sound of Colly's loud, excited voice neared the garage area, Benny dropped her hands and lifted the tire again. Marbeth rubbed at the slight print of his hands on her skin while Colly stopped just outside talking to a strange man in a white nylon windbreaker. Just looking at it made her hotter, and when the man turned to get out of Benny's way, she saw that the logo on the back of the jacket was from the Christian gas station, the one with the big wooden cross made out of four-by-fours on little metal rollers resting in the weeds beside the office. Born-again men and boys took turns dragging it around town while their fellow believers read Bible passages to them.

"When I got into turn four, it started to roll loose and I had to jump off the throttle," Colly was explaining. "Otherwise, the setup was so good, we knew we was gonna win tonight." He glanced at her, but his face was too shadowed to see the expression. "God willing, of course," he dropped his eyes.

Benny came in, took the next tire down, and paused with his back to the doorway. "Here we go again."

Sure, she sighed, and now she was in the suck-up position again. That's what she was good at.

"Well, I hate to see him hurt, but I'd like to see him smarter." Benny rolled the tire around her in a tight circle that left a cloudy smell she had to push through when Colly dropped his hand to his side where the man couldn't see it and motioned for her to come on out there.

The First Obligation

It wasn't easy being the side man. Homer was the uncomplaining sort though, which made him about perfect for the job of standing on the shoulder of the country road with the Dawson Garage tow truck parked in front of the '83 Buick belonging to Doris, Hill's widow. Homer's nearly new Dodge pickup was guarding the rear of the car a few yards back, while Senior was ragging on Junior again, had him under the Buick. Any idiot could see the jacks weren't set right, but the side man, well, he could only suggest certain things and sit around waiting for the disaster he was going to pick up after. That was his job. Homer was named after his uncle instead of his dad, who got to Lord knew where—his ma never said. Homer always believed his name was to remind her of baseball and the picture of Dad in his uniform playing American Legion ball one-handed after he got home from the service. The war took half his arm and the rest of his sense, was all Grandma Harriet would say. They were both of them women men ran off on. His mother and her mother. Kay, his girlfriend, said this town was full of after-being-a-wife women. She should know. Bobby Dunlop run on her twenty-five and a half years ago and she was not about to commit the same group of errors that got her in that position again. They'd been dating that long. Twenty-five years. Homer was her rebound, and after him she never needed another man. Honey, doesn't that mean something? he used to beg, but quit that ten years ago. He was the side man, nobody made a big decision in his direction.

The way the left front jack was leaning wasn't right, but if he said something, Daws Sr. was going to blow up and kick the car which would only make it worse. Puny stock jacks anyways, should've used the winch on the truck. Despite the rust eaten panels, that was a big heavy station wagon with enough newspapers in it to line the bird cages and cat boxes of everyone in this entire county. Hill's widow delivered the weekly on Saturdays. Every time one of Merle's garbage trucks rumbled past on the way to the town dump, the car shivered and the jack tilted some more. It was on gravel too. Thought he taught these boys better. Hadn't had a rain in so long, the shoulder was slick as asphalt. Nothing to hold that jack for long. The wind gusted down the road chasing some more of the cottonwood leaves their way and rocking the car. Daws Sr. looked across the hood at Homer and shook his head. Junior was messing up again. Just by being here instead of Rockingham or Charlottesville or Darlington Motor Speedways with the old man running the show from the sidelines, he'd messed up. Homer tried. Daws, he said, you were a genius behind the wheel. A natural. Junior is his own person though. I know, he won't even try, but it's not in his nature. Not everyone wants to compete. There's a cost to taking possession of that world. You should know that. Homer wanted to add that he never wanted it either. If anything, Junior was more his than Daws Sr.'s.

"It's not the oil pan." Junior's voice was muffled like he'd got a mouthful of dead leaves or old bread.

"Never said it was, for chrissakes, check the fuel line." Senior shoved his hands in his brown jumper pockets so hard Homer could hear the tear. Senior had those big hands that broke and ripped what they touched if he wasn't careful. Homer used to feel sorry for Marian, God rest her soul, being married to this much temperament. But then, turned out she had her own. Up and died of it. It was a wonder Junior wasn't a basket case walking around with half of each of those two in him. Well, Junior got his own cross to bear with that wife of his. A person could see from the get-go she was too much for a boy like Junior, but the kid had done pretty well under the circumstances. A good-looking woman with a brain and more ambition than a sprint car driver, it was pretty obvious Missy wasn't going to be cutting hair at the Curl Up & Dye for too long. So now she'd got herself a real estate license and a job working at Floyd Diehardt's insurance downtown there. She was bump drafting in the upper groove with her eye on the lead and not on Junior, who was right now flat on his back with some kind of fluid dripping on his face. Homer could see it when he stooped down for a minute and watched. Junior had the kind of hands a mechanic needed, just the right amount of feel for the little holes and hairline breaks in hoses and seams. Strong though, they were strong hands, could crack a rusted nut loose or pound out a fender. Senior's hands, a person had to be careful around.

Homer stood up just in time to see the blackbirds collecting in the muddy, torn-down field across the road lift like the edge of a hand, gather into a ball over the shoulder and ditch, whirl in a giant circle, then straighten and flow over the road.

"Found something," Junior called in that calm voice that about irritated Senior to death. It was like they traded places in life, Senior the jumpy impatient kid to Junior's slow, patient papa. Though Junior had married that woman, and Homer figured that had to go for something not seen on the surface with that boy. Kay said Junior was going to need her handbook before too long. The one she wrote for after-wives. She'd been trying to get someone to publish it in a regular store edition. She did it up at Neil's Copy Rite where she worked, and it looked nice, Homer told her. He happened to like that spiral binding and big print, made it easy to follow. A manual should be easy to follow, he told her. She didn't ask his advice though, she was more like Missy or Senior in that department. Gun it and plow on through before you got shuffled out of the draft. That was what they said on super speedways like Atlanta and Michigan.

There were a lot of days Homer had felt like quitting Dawson's racing team. Sunday afternoons he'd watch Senior go into backfield traffic, see the car skitter and twitch getting ready to collect the wall, he'd start praying, no, please Lord, do not let that fool think he can jam that car into that tiny hole, no, no—Senior had all the talent in the world. He really did, and Homer didn't just say that because he was the side man, as Kay called him. Senior had it all except the thing Junior had, and maybe that was why the old man was so damnably hard on the boy. Daws still had something to prove, especially after Pocono. What's-his-name, Bernilli's theorem be damned, the roof flaps didn't stop the car from going airborne. It was lucky he still had enough looks under that scar tissue to get another woman.

"Well, follow the leak back, for chrissakes, do I have to get under there myself?" Senior paced to the back of the car, rested a hand possessively on the gray cream roof pocked from the hail they had in July, and looked at Homer who shrugged. Senior came on around to where he was standing. "What'd you think?" he asked, lifting his stained, red-and-white Pennzoil hat and combing at his thick gray crew cut as if it'd grown long again.

"I think that jack is popping out." Homer used his boot to point at the one that was leaning. "Car's gonna fall."

"He's about done." Senior put his dirty thumbnail in his mouth and gave it a quick clean with his teeth. Marian used to make sure he cleaned up, but he was more careless now, unless he had a date. He could still charm the lug nuts off a wheel. That was part of Homer's job in the old days, keeping the women off. He did it for both of them—him and Marian. Senior didn't have the time and she didn't have the strength. Ate a hole in her stomach sitting there weekends watching him through qualifying, Happy Hour, and then the race. A hole that went all the way through her heart, Homer figured. It took her will to live, watching her husband's impatience wreck cars. Sometimes Homer would see her squeeze that baby so hard, Junior had marks where her nails bit into his fat little arms. The kid never cried though, eyes big as shift knobs, he'd sit there with cotton stuffed in his ears, watching and wait-ing. No wonder Junior was like he was today.

The car groaned as it got hit by a sideways gust of wind from another dump truck.

"Junior—" Homer tried to keep his voice calm. The boy was lying sideways on his shoulder fiddling with something halfway back.

"Let him finish, Homer," Senior took another nail down and spit dirt out. Kay said Senior would be divorced now if Marian hadn't passed when she did. A person had to wonder, but Homer defended Daws, saying she didn't know the whole story. None of them did. And that was the truth. There was love between the two of them, maybe just as impatient in its skin as Daws was, but it was there. Not a love like Homer had with Kay. Nor Junior with his wife. But a love that ate both of them alive, Homer figured. It would never have let them get checkered tablecloth comfort. He often wondered if it was her driving him to it, that racing busi-ness, her as much as him, because on days she couldn't make it, Senior did race more carefully, as if he had to get home to her, or as if it wasn't worth it to crash when she wasn't around to appre-ciate it. A person never knew.

The car groaned again. If it was his son, his flesh and blood, Homer would sure as shooting pull his ass out of there right now. "Daws—" He pointed at the jack this time.

"You about done there?" Senior walked around to the bumper hanging off the front there from when Hill's widow got it caught on the guardrail parking at the A&P. That was fun trying to unhook her that day. Kay said Hill's widow was not an after-wife. It wasn't the same. Doris, that was her name, but Homer always thought of her as Hill's widow to keep the story straight in his mind when Daws dragged him out on a call like this. They could just as well have hooked it up and pulled it into the garage, except she was sitting there in the tow truck and Senior liked to play the big man. Should have seen her eyes when they used the second jack. As bright-blue excited as this October sky.

"Dad?" Junior called out. "Can you get me the wrench and some duct tape?"

"You found it? What's wrong with it?" Squatting down close to the car, Senior's foot turned on a rock, and he reached up to steady himself on the door—it was all instinct—and the front jack gave a final squeal and let go.

Daws Sr. fell back as the car wobbled on the other jack at the rear and Homer yelled, "Junior get out!" But the car was already on its way down, landing with a big whump and sigh.

"Jesus Christ, Junior!" Homer ran to the other side and found him squirming out. When he grabbed his arm, the kid cried out, so Homer pulled on the back of the jumper, half strangling him, but it worked. Junior just lay there, holding the arm like something was broken, eyes shut, mouth tight. He was hurting.

"You hurt?" Senior asked like a blind man. The wind blew up under his cap, but he saved it just as it lifted off.

Junior rolled onto his other shoulder and gathered his legs up and raised himself to a sitting position. His face was pale and sweaty, and Homer wondered if the kid was in shock. He squatted down. "You break something?"

He squeezed his eyes shut and shook his head. "Shoulder's out," he panted.

"Well stand up here so we can pop it in." Senior could sound worse than he was. It was the relief of seeing his son okay that made him like this. He was not a man to baby a person when he couldn't baby himself. Still, Homer hoped the Hill widow knew what she was getting into. The wind threw some grit and leaves that stung his eyes to tears.

Homer helped Junior to his feet and held him against the car while his father yanked the arm and the shoulder popped back into place with a sound that made the stomach flop up and down like a trapped toad. They'd been through this before, when the kid was trying to play football and the thing popped out regular enough even the coach decided it wasn't worth it and dropped him from the team. Homer could tell Daws felt like maybe Junior was doing it on purpose to avoid working hard, and there was a brief glimmer of that in Senior's eyes now, but it went away as he remembered he was the one dropped the car on his son. No apology though, a person would have to wait till their dog talked for an apology from Daws Senior. He made up for it by acting like nothing happened, telling a joke maybe. Then it was so damn awkward a person had to forgive him just to get back to normal. Nothing like a man trying to be what he wasn't, Homer knew. That was where all the trouble of the world came from.

There was a grid of black grease marks along Junior's shoulder and sleeve where the car fell on him, and he winced as he gave his arm a couple of tentative turns to see if it was working right.

"You get it figured out?" Senior asked.

"Yeah." Junior leaned his head back, closed his eyes and twisted his neck until it cracked a couple of times.

"What's holding us up then?" The wind sneaked in the back window of the Buick and rattled the papers around good before running out the other window.

Junior looked at his dad, they were both tall, the same square shoulder build and height, eye to eye, except the jittery thing in the dad disappeared in the space between the two. They had these eyes, brown with a kind of gold backlight, that people noticed. They're beautiful eyes, Kay said, they make all kinds of promises. Daws could just look at Marian sometimes and she'd calm right down. Junior got that girl he married by keeping his mouth shut and using his eyes on her. That was her only mistake, thinking the kid was all that. Even at fifty-six years old, Daws could flash those eyes at women and they smiled. He was the kind of person could make you happy or sad with a look. But it was a different matter the two of them looking at each other.

Homer couldn't help it. He saw those bits of dry grass and leaf on the kid's back and brushed at them. He could feel Senior's eyes on the side of his face, and sighed. Daws would think Homer was betraying him again, taking his son's side. One of Merle's trash trucks barreled by, shaking the car and throwing gravel at them.

"I'm hauling it back to the garage." Junior flexed his shoulder again and there was that sickening grind. He was supposed to have surgery years ago, but he wouldn't. Homer didn't know how he stood it.

Senior opened his mouth to protest, then stopped and put his hand on the roof of the car, looking at the good truck where Doris Hill sat waiting. A smile parted his lips and he shook his head and looked at the ground, scuffed his shoe through the gravel and dirt and shrugged. "Homer can ride with you in the tow truck. I'll take Mrs. Hill in his truck." They nodded and went to work. The old man had shuffled his work their way again. Junior and Homer were going bowling tonight though, and they didn't want to waste the rest of the day out on the road arguing. Besides, Homer was the side man, just along for the ride.

IS IT TOO MUCH TO ASK?

That's what I keep saying to myself, and you know the answer. So every morning I put a green dot on the calendar day if it's racing weather and a red one if it's not and a yellow for caution, rain or snow expected. A habit I picked up as a kid. Then I wash up and go into the kitchen and pull out the box of seven-grain oatmeal. But today there's a surprise. I open the new box and shake and nothing comes out. I tear the flap back more and shake and nothing happens. This time I look inside. Alien oatmeal. The top is covered in a thick gray tent with little spikes of grain sticking out. Nothing moving. I quick dump the whole thing in the garbage.

I know, I should take it back to the A&P. You take your chances, I tell my son. Maybe I've said it too often though, because as far as I can tell he's a person will die without having taken one single chance his whole life. But I'll tell you, that oatmeal set the tone for the whole day. Then Doris's station wagon springs some kind of problem out on the county road to the dump, and Junior and I go whizzing out there in the tow truck and he lets the whole damn car fall on him. Right in front of Homer too. Not that he's hurt. That shoulder pops out at a blink. Should've had surgery but when the doc a few years ago tells him there's a twenty percent chance it'll be worse after that, he won't do it. That's the kind of son I have.

And Homer. No point trying to explain anything to Homer, who's blamed me for every single thing that's happened since Marian died. Hell, he was blaming me for getting her pregnant before she even told me.

And he always takes the kid's side of things. Used to do it for me when we were younger, but now it's like he's lost his memory of the good things in life. Hangs around that dingbat Kay from the copy place and follows Junior around. Hell, I thought we could take a quick look-see under the Buick. I didn't check the jacks, personally, I mean Junior practically grew up under cars. He's a grown man, that's what I should've said when Homer held the kid down on the car and gave me the fish eye while I snapped the shoulder back in place. It's not like I wasn't sorry to see him hurt again, but a man gets tired of it.

I didn't even debate using that oatmeal. That worries me. In the old days, when Junior was still around, I would've shoveled off that top layer and found the good stuff at the bottom of the box. Boiling kills about anything that crawls.

Doris had to borrow my pickup to finish delivering the weekly, and I had to go with her to drive. She drives like such a maniac, makes me look like a paralytic nun behind the wheel. No wonder she tore the bottom outta that wagon. Don't bother fixing it, I told her, with your money you can afford a new one. She always thinks she's broke so it don't do any good. She'll show up with another loser she's bought off Chick's Used and Reconditioned New Cars. What the hell is that—either it's new or not, I tell him, but he just cracks his knuckles or jingles the change in his pocket and smiles. Best year Chick ever had, he bought himself that pink doublewide and parked it behind the lot on the edge of town where people know they can get a dollar or two for the last couple of broken-down miles their car has in it. Here in Iowa, with the bad country roads and miles you have to go just to see a movie or grab a decent bite to eat, we generally drive the piss out of our vehicles. Chick's cars get a down-and-dirty paint job and good interior cleaning, then pop up again in your rearview mirror for a few more laps before they spin away, engines blown, chassis broke apart. So enough said.

Doris listens to Chick because he was her dead husband Roger's buddy in high school. That's too far back for most of us to pay any mind, but Doris is loyal after her fashion, though lately I've come to suspect that she might be getting more than a bad used car from Chick. Who goes driving you all over the damn county with those weeklies, I want to ask her. But it's too late to start in now. Besides, if I was to start in on somebody, it'd have to be my son.

Anyway, I let Doris take the truck home to get dressed after she dropped me off. So I get dressed and hear something come clanking through the mail slot. Here it is:

HELLO NEIGHBORS,

After reading the letters from some of my neighbors and realizing and understanding their concerns, I would like to add more problems to that list. Here are some of the problems that have been happening to me for the last two years.

—My 1981 Chev. mysteriously caught on fire and burned beyond repair, early one morning.
—Small rocks, acorns and tennis balls are thrown at my home, close to my bedroom window, after midnight. I have picked up between twenty and thirty balls out of my yard.
—Small rocks are thrown on my roof, I can hear then rolling down and off.
—Eggs thrown at my garage. (Very difficult to scrub off.)
—Knocking on my bedroom window at night and window peeking.
—Ringing of both front and side doorbells, several times, late at night.

—Dismantling of the rain gutters.

I feel that each and every one of us should become more conscious and vigilant of our neighborhood to help reduce these problems. Thanks!

—A Concerned Resident Of Bedford Ave.

I turn the page over and then reread it before going outside to check the neighborhood. Some new people moved in last year, one family down the block with lots of kids and the couple next door with nothing but a fancy Ford Explorer they take care of like it's a relative. I know who sent the letter. I can see her white aluminum-sided house across the street with the locked cyclone fence so the mailman has to dump her mail in the stand alone box by leaning over as far as his arms will reach. I could go over there and explain electrical shorts in engines to her. Tell her that it's pretty damn natural for acorns to drop on your house if there's a big oak tree in the neighbor's yard, and balls and rocks come just as naturally out of the hands of little boys. Same with window peeking. The rain gutters have me stumped though.

I go around the yard kicking at the big yellow and brown sycamore leaves instead, thinking maybe I should rake a few while I'm waiting for Doris, but I don't want to sweat up my good shirt because she'll notice and maybe want to go home early.

She's a cat lover, that's the problem. I don't like 'em. Like now, that black and white comes prowling along the edge of the house behind the arborvitae, thinking I don't see him so he can spray my door again and get every damn stray in town yowling out here half the night. I try to stay casual as I walk toward the bushes, scuffing leaves up with the toes of my shoes, not looking in his direction as I ball my pocketknife in my fist. The cat freezes with his front paw up, pointing like a dog at the cement steps. I shoot the knife at him. It only makes a little thump because it's not open, and the cat hisses and leaps across the steps and away.

Doris would have a fit if she saw me. She has this cat Vincent. Another thing I hate about cat people, they think it's endearing to call girls boy names and so on. But I figure at fourteen, it doesn't have a lot of time left. Should've died long ago of embarrassment, but cats don't seem to have much pride, at least not the kind people claim they have. Doris tries to convince me that Vincent can act just like a dog—she's trained it to go on a leash, fetch a ball, and hunt. Last week, she showed me the obituary she's written up for when Vincent "is called." The weekly will print it, she's assured me. I bet they will. Twenty dollars and you could say grace over a pan of biscuits if you wanted. The obit is two pages long. Who the hell has that much to say about a cat? Mario Andretti won't get that much coverage.

One thing Marian always liked about living here, the neighborhood's quiet this time of evening. Good place to raise the kid. People eating in front of the TVs make the windows glow this eerie blue. Couch potatoes. They better be careful these days. There was that guy in California came home from work and lay on that couch so long the family decided to kill him. He wasn't helping, they said. "I wanted to do it, but I didn't want to do it," the wife said. "Like I said, he was a miserable bastard, but he had his good points too." Something about that makes me feel bad, like maybe Marian, my wife who passed several years ago, would say about me if she were around now. I didn't mean not to be good to her, it's not something you plan out if you're a man, it just sort of happens. I don't know, if I lived in one of these other houses along the street, I'd be looking at my family a little differently after a story like that.

They were just poor, Doris said when I told her. Poor doesn't turn you into a murderer, I said. Then that Vincent cat thumped onto the bed and nudged its fat way onto her chest so I got dressed and went home. That was two nights ago.

The houses are one story on this block, the tail end of the street where the money ran out in the forties after the war. I promised Marian a lot of things in our life, one was a big house, but we only got this far. Another was that I'd go to church with her as soon as my racing was done, but after the fire, I never felt much like talking to anybody about God's plans. I suppose she'd be happy to see me in my dark blue suit jacket, white shirt, and gray pants tonight, tie hanging on the doorknob for when Doris shows up so she can put the knot right.

We're going to the visitation for Sister Dionysia before we go to dinner at the bowling alley. They have this Saturday night all-you-can-eat chicken buffet until eight, and if she doesn't hurry we're going to miss it. Something about the idea of missing the buffet claws right at me. I hate to see dead people on an empty stomach. Sister Dionysia was her mother's sister who joined the order in Minnesota but got shipped out when she went a little too crazy. It was her camping in the abandoned car across from the Mother House that prompted the call to the police, I guess, and then she fell in the cell and hit her head so hard, and they didn't catch the pneumonia in time. It's not like Doris knew her, but I didn't put up much of a stink because that damn Chick probably would've taken her if I didn't. If Junior was any kind of a son, he'd let me drive his car tonight. All I've got is the garage pickup until I get enough money to drop a new motor in the Trans Am. I suppose he's all unhappy about the car this afternoon. It was an accident, my foot slipped, I've never hurt him on purpose. But the way Homer looked at me—

The sky's dripping pink all over the place, and the wind's died down from this afternoon. You can feel that chill that comes when the fall sun goes, it settles all over my wool suit jacket and between the whiskers on my face. I shaved this morning, but it comes in so fast. When I first started seeing Doris, I'd shave twice a day. Chick is bald, I mean bowling-ball bald. In fact, his whole body is bald. Last night on the phone after she broke our date, I told Doris it was unnatural to have no hair. He must be an alien or something. She ignored me like maybe he had hair in places I couldn't see, and that made me mad so I had to say yes to going to the visitation and seeing dead people before dinner, and picking her up when her car broke on the road to the dump. What was she doing out that way? I take one last glance around the small yard, nod at the grass that's still bright fertilizer green, and go inside. The house has trapped enough day heat to make it seem stuffy, though by the time I come home later it will have that cold that'll only get colder. Doris won't spend the night here until after the fifteenth when I finally turn the heat on.

Why the road to the dump where there aren't any houses? I go to the mantel over the fake gas grate and dust the top of each picture frame with my hand. There I am in the red-and-white car, there I am winning an ARCA race, and those two in the BGN series, and here, the time I made the top five in Winston Cup at Darlington. Marian's at my side in each one, her small thin arms around my waist, her head about touching my collarbone or standing separate with Junior in her arms and mine draped across her shoulders. She's smiling and frowning both, and the baby just stares.

Krohn's disease. She kept losing weight from the pain that they kept getting wrong. Then there was the bleeding and diarrhea, finally the really bad infection that finished her. I feel like I want to remember something about her that isn't a sum of these parts of our life, cars and the hospital stays, but I can't. I look around the living room at the brown sectional and blue plaid wingback that was always more hers than mine while I was mostly gone racing. And I guess that's why I finally live in defeat, so full of anger that my son and my only friend act like my gear ratios are always wrong. Marian kept all our good days inside her, she knew how to remind me what they were, those things I miss now, and when she left, it was just Junior and me like two blank walls facing each other. Marian keeps us apart now. She's between us, with all the time we spent as husband and wife and son sealed up in reserve against me. Is it too much to ask that someone see this?

My neighbor across the street, sending these nutso letters, she's so lonely she's seeing things, Homer's blaming me for trying to kill my kid, and my kid, he's married to that girl will barely speak to him or me—a person has to wonder. I mean a whole life can't come down to this collection of furniture and photographs, like a bunch of trophies you win in go-cart for just showing up—what kind of a race is that? I mean the sun's going down, my car engine's blown, and I can't even remember enough of my life to cry good tears over it. I feel like I'm rolling loose, about to hit the wall again, and no one's looking anymore.

SOMEWHERE BETWEEN CAUSE AND EFFECT

"It's the same reason you're here bowling." Missy tossed her head and took another swig off the longneck. It was so cramped sitting side by side at the little scoring table, Daws had to drink with his left hand to match her beer for beer, even though it hurt his shoulder every time he lifted the bottle.

"You do everything because your daddy did it. You don't even like bowling. Look at the way you get up there and just toss it down the lane. You're not even looking half the time."

"Not a matter of like, darlin'. We're rednecks, that's why we bowl." He drained the grainy bottom of the bottle and watched Homer and Kay put the finishing touches on their turns to beat them at another game. The older couple gave each other high fives and came back to check their scores with new swagger in their thick hips.

"You're buying." Homer clapped Daws's sore shoulder where the car had dropped off the jack on him this morning. Another red-letter racing day.

"Wanna just surrender your wallet now or you getting to like the slow pain?" Homer grinned, his tongue jiggling the upper bridge of teeth, a habit he'd had for as long as Daws could remember. Another casualty of his dad's car wars, only Homer wouldn't see it that way. Daws peeled the scoring page off and handed it to him as Missy started the new column.

"I'll get the beer." Daws stood, letting his cramped lower back muscles take up an extra stitch of pain before he collected the empties and headed for the bar-restaurant over in the far corner. The ache in his shoulder started a pulse that tightened all the way up his neck and across the top of his scalp. No wonder he was losing hair in his late twenties. In the early days when Missy used to wash it, she'd massage his whole head until he felt relaxed enough to let go of the jaw muscles he hadn't been aware he was holding until that moment. It embarrassed him. A person should know his own body better than that.

It was Couples Saturday Night at the Golden Bowl and Lounge, and all along the lanes clusters of men and women gathered, laughing and shouting to be heard over the din of thumping balls, clattering pins, and oldies music that Cyrus piped in on these nights. Friday it was country music and Tuesday, Wednesday, and Thursday contemporary hard rock for the bowling leagues. Dawson wondered what he played during the day when the alley was taken over by women and kids. It was usually so damn noisy you couldn't hear the lyrics anyway.

Nick, the guy from the Big Wheel parts store, looked up and nodded at him, and he waggled two empties his direction. The guy wanted Daws to help him get on a Winston Cup pit crew. Hell, Daws couldn't help anybody do anything, but the guy was a persistent son of a bitch. Kept wanting to go out after work for a beer and burger. Most nights Daws was lucky to limp home from work on his own two feet. Old man said he had to earn his way one way or another eight years ago, and they both knew what it meant when the Coke can hit the wall and exploded over the old red and white number seven car draped with cloudy plastic in the corner of the garage.

Daws took a deep breath of air and opened the dirty glass door to the bar-restaurant at the far end of the building, releasing the stale steam of old cigarette smoke, beer, grease, and pine cleanser. The long knotty pine bar and cigarette scarred black tables were packed with people standing two and three deep, drinking and trying to be heard over the music. He pushed his way through to the end of the bar where the black-haired waitress was lifting off a big tray of drinks, her wide sweaty face set in stoical lines.

" 'Scuse me." He leaned awkwardly away from the tray and she gave him a look that could peel paint off a car. He remembered her then, Carla, a girl he'd gone to high school with. They hadn't had much to say to each other since that night sophomore year at the quarry. He took her place at the end of the bar looking in the mirror while he waited for the bartender to slide his way. In the neon smoky light his brown hair and regular features looked about like Jeff Gordon's, the young Winston Cup star people sometimes mistook him for. Well, not that they made a huge mistake, mostly they said he reminded them of Jeff. "Near-beer," his dad snorted one time, and Daws had stung for weeks afterward. When the bartender looked his way, he held up the four empties and the guy nodded. More people seemed to crowd in against him, bumping his sore shoulder into another round of aching. Maybe he should see a doctor Monday. Have to take off the morning, which would piss off the old man who already saw him as the hole their good racing name fell into.

"What's happening?" He asked when the bartender set the four cold ones down.

"Moonlight Madness. Gimmick Cyrus come up with. Glow-in-the-dark bowling. Goes on in—" the bartender looked at the Miller Lite clock over the door, "fifteen minutes, ten o'clock. Need to get your glow tape for shirts and shoes at the desk. He already taped the rental shoes." He swept up the seven dollars Daws laid on the bar and mouthed thanks.

Daws decided to go to the desk first to get the tape so they could bowl more games. No point in going someplace else now. He wondered how he'd missed the promotion coming in three hours earlier. There were several people lined up ahead of him, apparently asking for the same tape and being refused in order to clear out the lanes for the crowd waiting in the bar. When his turn came, he set the bottles down decisively and took out his wallet. "How much?" he asked before Cyrus could shake his head.

Cyrus had a ten-year-old kid who wanted to do more than race his go-cart around the Midwest, and somehow he had come to believe along with everyone else that Daws, because of his dad's one brush with fame, could help get his kid up the next rung on the ladder. Daws watched this thought creep across the man's face. In a slow flush of recognition, Cyrus let a grin break through that didn't match his washed-out blue eyes or thin mouth. He ran his hand across the top of his bald head as if it were covered with invisible hair.

"No problem—just take and put some of this tape on your shirt and shoes if they're your own." He looked at his watch. "Lights go out in about ten minutes."

"Thanks." Daws dropped the roll of tape in the pocket of his black T-shirt and picked up the bottles as Cyrus opened his mouth to say something else. "Thanks again." He turned away quickly enough that the shoulder twinged again. Damn car wasn't up on the jack right. He'd seen that but crawled under it anyway. Something about an oil or gas leak, and he hadn't wanted to look like a chicken in front of Daws Sr. It was the old man had the connection to racing, he should tell Cyrus. Hell, Dawson Jr. was just along for the ride. His life didn't mean spit in the rain most days. But it was like that Bob Feller deal, he decided as he walked down the stained blue-and-red flecked carpet toward the far end where the others waited. Most people were so shy, they got their biggest kick out of talking to someone who knew Bob Feller rather than Bob himself. Maybe he should open a museum for his dad's stuff like they did in Van Meter, Bob's hometown north of here. Except the old man wouldn't have it.

He put down the beers and held up the tape. "Glow-in-the-dark bowling, have to wear some of this if we're going to stay. Where do you want it Homer, your mouth?" He tore a piece off and tried to stick it on the front of Missy's navy silk blouse she'd worn to work this morning at the insurance office, but she pushed his hand away, which was about normal these days. "Lights out and we won't be able to find you, honey." He plastered the tape vertically on his black sleeve and tore another piece. This one he put in a line down the front of his shirt.

"Here—let me." Homer grabbed the tape and tore two quick pieces off and stuck them in an x on the left front of his own tan sports shirt, then repeated the action on the right so it looked like he was covering his nipples. "Once more," he tore two bigger pieces and stuck them to the bulging front of his chocolate-brown polyester pants.

"Give me that." Kay, his girlfriend of twenty-five years, grabbed the tape and put two pieces on his back, then followed with a couple on her shirt and shoes before handing it back to Missy.

"Alright," Missy sighed and carefully tore several pieces. "Make a star," she ordered, and handing Daws the first piece, turned her back. When he lifted her thin blonde hair off her neck, she said, "No, do it right there in the middle where it can be seen." When he was done, the lopsided star looked like it was drunk on the navy background, but he didn't tell her that.

"What about your back?" she asked, putting a strip on her sleeve.

He was about to tell her just to put another stripe, when Homer grabbed the tape. "I got it—" A long one down and a short one across. Dawson knew what it was before Homer clapped his bad shoulder again. "Number seven, nobody's gonna miss you now, boy."

"Brilliant." Missy took a slug off her beer. "We playing or what?" There was no pleasing her either since he'd made it plain and clear his end of the family business was to be conducted on his back under cars. She'd moved from hairdressing to selling insurance as soon as she got his last name tacked to hers five years ago, but things had stalled since then. He had no idea how much longer she was staying.

"Better do our shoes before the lights go out," Kay said.

It was as if he could feel the seven like a scar on his back, and he turned away before the others could see it on his face. He'd grown up with seven being the big magic number in the house. Everything was seven, or some multiple, for his dad's racing luck, and when he was little he learned to hate other numbers that threatened seven—like eight and twenty-nine, anything with six. Eleven. Ten. Three. "Your son is having trouble in arithmetic," his third-grade teacher had written on the report card. Then gradually he began to hate the number seven too.

"Seven come eleven." Homer grinned and started to punch his sore shoulder again, but Daws stepped out of the way. That had been the battle cry when Homer had helped his dad in the pits. Hell, Cyrus should get Homer to help his kid. That old fart still kept track of half the racing world. Unlike Daws Sr. or his mother who finally put a stop to the whole business after she developed problems with her colon from sitting on the sidelines and holding her breath for hours at a time while her husband tried to kill himself. That was her view. And after the car had come rolling loose in turn two at Pocono, Daws Sr. had agreed. There was still an awful lot of scarring along his face and chest and hands from the fire. Nowadays the drivers wore these flame retardant suits that gave them an extra fifteen or twenty seconds. And elaborate helmets and custom-made driver's chairs to keep them safe in the roll cages. He'd never forget the image of his father's body bursting into flame, as if he had self-combusted as he fell out of the window onto the track, where the spilled fuel was burning like a long sun-colored tail from the wrecked car.

"When're you going racing, son?" people in town used to ask him. Later they just looked at him like he was chicken.

When the lights went out, there was a moment of utter darkness and quiet, then the music burst back on and sucked their breath up into a noisy explosion of laughter and shouting. The automatic setters lifted and clanked down a new set of pins that glowed like misshapen mushroom faces at the end of the lanes. The only color in the dark came from the neon signs over the lanes and along the walls, the greenish glow tape outlining each lane and the faint orange and blue tints of the balls.

"Come here, Fred Astaire," Kay laughed, and a big x appeared on Homer's back as he spun once and lost his balance, crashing into the scoring table and knocking over one of the beers which

Missy quickly scooped up. They all held their hands up, squinting at their shapes.

"What now?" Kay asked, and the lanes around them began to thump and pound and clatter again.

"You losers go first." Homer's voice seemed to float across a space made larger, more empty in the darkness.

"I'm going." Daws looked at his feet to make sure they were down there, reassured by the glowing stripes. When he walked he felt narrowed, like a table knife, as if the rest of him had been cut and trimmed away. He found the button for the blower and pushed it, feeling for the burst of hot air to dry his hands. Then he had to put his fingers in all the holes and lift every ball before he could figure out which one was his. Cyrus had some work to do on the logistics here, he thought as he hefted the ball in his two hands ignoring the shoulder. The weight felt strange, awkward, and off balance as if it were holding him, and as he looked down the lane at the pins glowing like huge noses, he felt the ball lead him forward two stumbling steps and lunge out of his hands to spin like a moon with uncontrollable force toward the end, which erupted in a splatter of jagged light. He stood there feeling dizzy until Missy put an arm around his waist.

"Good going. My turn."

As he watched, his wife walked calmly through her routine as if the lights were on, getting her usual knockdown with a spare. He looked at the board over the lane for the first time that evening and saw the number five flashing. When she caught the spare, the star on her back winking like a directional signal under her long hair, the number disappeared in the dark. Suddenly she was next to him again, and he couldn't quite recognize her in the dim light. Her thin face had these new angles, sharper and somehow uglier. She seemed to leer at him, and he kept having to look away. Her small teeth seemed neon for some reason. He'd had the same sensation other times, like when they were first married and used to drink too much and he couldn't stand to have her touch him. One time she'd sat up in bed and said,

"You're deformed, Dawson," as if he'd accused her out loud of something terrible. When he'd pressed her later, sober, she'd told him it was nothing, forget it, but he hadn't.

"Your father has an agreement with fate," his mother had said from the hospital bed that time she was bleeding so bad. "He thinks nothing bad can happen."

At the scoring table he found what he thought was his beer and took a long pull then spit part of it back. He didn't want to walk all the way to the bar in the dark for more. Missy sat down and kicked his bowling shoe and he felt it all the way up his leg, not as pain but as disturbance. "How ya doing?" She grinned and those teeth looked harmless as a saw blade hanging on the wall. He nodded and realized she might not see it.

"You're getting weirder by the day, you know that?" She stood up close and leaned her face into his like an evil jack-o'-lantern. He looked around at the slashes of light moving erratically across the dark, the balls of light rolling in symmetrical arcs toward their final destination, the human voices suddenly a din of noise as strident and jagged as the light itself, breaking the even darkness of the room as if that were the sole reason for their being here.

"I don't know what to do," he'd said to his mother that time in the hospital when they'd almost lost her. He was sixteen and his father had quit racing himself but set up the shop for his son's racing career and his dream of the years to come. Daws Jr. had tried to explain to his mother that it was the numbers, the way the seconds and splits, the speeds, the RPMs, the gear ratios and points, all those numbers spun and twisted in his head like a knife he'd swallowed at birth that just grew and grew to fill his whole body until he couldn't get away from its point held to the softest part of his brain.

"A dream is something you die for," she'd told him, and he'd looked at her, lying there drained of blood as if her own dream and not his father's was the thing he should fear. He'd understood then that she loved her husband, that his father hadn't forced her to what was her death bed, she had climbed into it herself. They were lucky, these two people, his parents, he'd come to realize over the next few years. Lucky because they'd been true to their dreams and because they knew what those dreams were. Recognized them out of all the others that must have presented themselves like dancers at the dance.

"Come on, seven." Homer didn't try to slap him on the shoulder this time, and when Daws looked at the other man, he saw the same confusion in the face that his must be wearing. In this disguise, none of them looked the same, their stories could all be false. They could all be demons, without any dreams except the ones that kept them from walking away when the old man might say something like crawl under that car. And what he really meant was that car's going to fall off the jack and you'll be lucky to get out with only a bruised shoulder and sore back, but next time, next time I'm gonna get you. The same demon that kept him from walking out on Missy, he guessed.

Daws stepped up to the trough of balls and ran his hands over the smooth circles of light, trying to feel for the one that had carried him to glory last time. When he found what he thought was the right one, he hefted its weight and let it carry him forward to the line once again. This time as he let it go, he felt his heart give this sad little jerk watching the ball in its orbit go down crashing at the end. But this time when all the numbers on the dark wall in front of him flashed three times for the strike, it was okay, they were just pieces of some puzzle that had come apart before the lights went out.

Flat Spotting

It's right after I flat spot the left front tire and it feels like driving with a board nailed on it. I'm trying to remember to race, but the concentration comes and goes. There's so much noise and I opened the car like a can of spam in back when L.F. and I mixed it up on the sixty-seventh, so I'm getting hit with dirt, rubber, oil, and smoke. It's like the inside of a vacuum cleaner, all that debris flying around. When I pitted that time, we cleaned it up some, but it didn't do much good. The rubber is like tarry gravel that sticks and I know I'm in for some nasty weather as cars keep passing me. It's my job though, to keep the car out here and show the sponsors' names so I do it, trying not to think about my lungs being black-lined and the fire I'll be sucking in sooner or later if those morons keep making me stand on the brakes every time they lap me.

So like I said, the left front is flat spotted and that puts the car loose and I don't want to pit again, so I think about something else as much as the car. The neighbor who made a pact with the devil has been threatening to come racing and I wonder if he's out there in the grandstand. Maybe throwing whatever power he has against me. Then Jimmy comes up on my bumper and nudges me to get by and the car takes it shivering and I sit on the inside for a bit more to let him know I'm still in the race, then move up, fighting the tire and the car that has no handling worth shit anymore. Wait till it's his turn, I think, not giving him more room than he needs. I don't mind making him scrape by. He'd been one of those early out boys causing all the trouble for the front runners two hundred some laps back.

Pulled the plug on the radio just before the last pit. Hate hearing their sanctimonious bullshit. I know I'm out of the race. I knew this job before they could spell car. Sloppy spotter, that's what led to the first tangle on turn two. Spun out three of us. Hit the oil on the track going 111—what the hell did he think that shadow was? I'll settle with him later. I'm okay, I told them, I'm okay. Shut the hell up, I wanted to say. So first chance I got, I pulled the plug. There wasn't time to fix it in the pit. I kept telling them I couldn't hear when they plugged it in again. Let them worry about that. By now the other drivers know, make them worry for a change, I decide. But Jimmy doesn't care, nor Blaze, nor a whole lot of others. We're racing. Even if I don't like the neighbor up there in the stands. Why couldn't he work his stuff on someone else?

Caution flag. Okay, good. Downshift, off the throttle, let the tires cool, maybe that left front won't go flat, that'd be the one break in this whole lousy day. No, I am not going to pit. I was just in there, I'm tired of those guys. Okay, alright alright.

I look at the crowd across the track, hoping to spot the neighbor while I wait out the tire changes and fuel and they're still banging away at that hole in back, tearing metal off, spot riveting and taping shit. All I can see are blots of color. I've been making circles on this short track so long everything seems to stick in place by comparison. Scooter has trouble with the jack like always, fumbling around back there, then he drops a tire on John's foot. Lucky I'm fifteen laps down or I'd have to take it up with him again. He practically cost us the race at Talladega, with his jerking around. He's trained with the other guys though, so we can't do much. Season's almost over. I'm going to blast out of here whether he's got that jack down or not. He'll learn to hustle after he's scraped a couple yards of concrete off his face. What the hell. Maybe the neighbor got to him. I look around wondering how many of my crew have made pacts with the devil to guarantee I don't place in the top ten this year.

Rusty and I drag race down pit row to get the heat up in the tires and I win and we're racing again. The caution's still on so I get in line at the very back and we go on parade while they try to clean up Marty's latest mess. Hell, Jean left him because he was going to kill too many people by the time he was done. He pulls that crap in front of me, I'm going to run right through him. He knows, I told him, he stays as far away as he can now. Jean went to racing on the ARCA circuit to save her life, she says. She's damn good. Rather have her in front of me than that idiot Marty. Blew up his engine again, taking Bobby with him when he spun. Most of us blow we manage to limp out of the way. Not that idiot. He's probably the one put the oil down, too. Too stupid to notice when the gauges get buried. He must've made a pact with the devil. He never gets hurt, just everybody around him. Yeah, they're medivacking Bobby. Son of a bitch.

I weave a little to get the heat up in the tires and notice how loose the car's getting. Should've told them to tighten it down again. Put some more wedge in. Thought it was the tires. This is going to be fun.

God, I hate how this shit from the hole in back keeps peppering me. Just got the visor cleaned at the last pit, and already it's like looking through chocolate. Uh oh, what's that? Shit, the clutch is going. Linkage. Okay, okay. I'm not going in to pit again. Just keep my foot on it a little, that's it. Happened at Michigan that time, I know what to do. Keep the mind off, we're three-fourths of the way through. We're on cruise control, billboard in motion. It's the damn decals holding this piece of crap together today anyhow. Wonder if that neighbor wants a spot, maybe the front bumper where I can push it right up somebody's ass. Marty's for instance.

Okay, we're racing. Jimmy's trying to get through again, damn hog. Wants every race now he's got eight under his name.

I had some seasons like that. We all did back here. You never think it'll be you, one of the field cars being nudged out of the way by a kid with nothing to lose. He doesn't hurt in enough places yet. They haven't built a special chair or steering wheel or pedals for all his broken pieces yet. But they will. Then he'll feel that shimmy and the car slipping up toward the wall. He'll be the one wondering if that black streak is his from last time or this time as he manages to hold it, hold it and come down again without hitting traffic and spinning the whole damn lot of you out.

My neighbor leaves his garage door up all night long, cars and bikes and water skis sprouting in there like a thieves' shopping mall. Kid stuff all over the driveway and front lawn. Hell, he brags he doesn't even lock his front door half the time. Nothing gets touched. My wife leaves the Explorer out front one night and in the morning, you guessed it, the stereo and airbags are ripped out of it. You ain't living right, Dar, that's what the guy says to me. I leave the garage open one afternoon while I run to the Ace Hardware down at Four Corners, you know they barely had time to turn around in front of the house, but they got the table saw. My kids' bikes disappear like they're being sucked up by martians. We practically have to chain them and the kids to the house. Not the neighbor. I find his kids wandering the streets half the night. Little kids. Nobody touches them though. That's how I know he's made the deal.

Shit, there's that new kid, Sput, Spout or something, steering that Pontiac like a grocery cart through the supermarket aisles. Wish I had a radio could blast into some of these assholes' headsets. What're you shopping for, dandruff shampoo? He's asleep, doesn't have a clue. Be lucky to make five races without putting his goods in a to-go bag. Stay back there, you little shit. I can't take the high line, I'm too loose. Don't you even think of coming inside me, not here, wait—Stand on the brakes, squaring the tires again, I can feel the flat spots—Oh no, oh no, oh don't do that, no! Son of a bitch, here we go, here we go—

* * *

I'm alright, I'm alright goddamn it, just get me out of here. It's hotter than hell. I think we're on fire, no, I can feel it, it's under me, goddamn it, pull the net off—there, that's good, now help me with this harness. Shit, thing's stuck, cut the fucker, cut it, I don't give a shit, come on, come on! Oh there, thanks man.

They're towing the car off and it's beat to hell. Ron's pissed, but it wasn't my fault, not this time. Soon as I get out of here, I'm going to find that Sput kid and put his hillbilly ass right back on that Georgia dirt track. Go-carts, that's what he must've been driving before this.

Oh no, here comes that neighbor, all smiles like he's selling insurance or running for office. Perfect. He's wearing a team hat. Meet my new sponsor, Ron says.

Well, why the hell not, maybe I can make a pact with you-know-who and win one of these goddamn things again.

What I'm Doing in Missouri

For years now I've been taking pictures for evidence of God's grace. These are the tornado destroyed houses of Moberly, the brick buildings shattered by a giant fist. Fires, the way the windows end up outlined with black as if they've been eating burnt marshmallows, a black lipped mouth hollering at the world. Okay, what are they saying, I ask. They never look like eyes to me, not when I see the side gutted like a deer, spilling appliances and curtains, the lath and plaster reaching out like an arm missing a ride.

Is all this destruction addressed to someone in particular? I ask God. Are you tearing Satan's kingdom down? What about the bodies of dumb animals squatting in the dust until the heat swells and bursts them open?

The phone call last night. He needs you.

I come from a long line of star-crossed lovers, so I know what it means to live in the aftermath of explosions. I've even thought of doing a special collector's edition of the family pictures. Audubon killed everything he drew, that's what I always figured love was like.

What time? I asked the voice on the other end of the line. When did it happen?

Great-great-aunt Esperance had stood in the swirling dust of her late August Missouri farmyard the afternoon the raiders rode up and asked for water. They were hungry too, and without asking, she ran to the shelves where the fresh baked bread sat cooling and brought it all, every loaf, and tubs of butter and mulberry jam to the men lying in the shade of the box-elder trees out by the potato patch. She said nothing as one man dug in the potato hills, pulling the brown lumps from the earth, shaking the dirt off and passing them around as if they were prized apples off the trees in the orchard. Which she would have given them too, had she not been watching the one in the brightly embroidered shirt whose cerulean blue thread caught the shade of his eyes and wove it around and over his shoulders and chest. In one fatal gesture, he refused the food and took her instead. Esperance was marrying age, but since all the men had been driven away or enlisted, she had been waiting for the bright arrival of this man.

After giving out the food—leaving only enough so the family could struggle through the cold spring months—Esperance climbed up behind the blue-eyed man and rode off to set up light housekeeping. No one married her until years and years later, but by then she'd already had the two children, who stayed small and brown as that potato he left beneath the box-elder, sprouting red eyes that watched the grief in the house grow.

Let me talk to him, I told the caller. Put Blu on the phone.

By the next summer, Esperance's mother and sisters were being shipped to prison in Springfield for supporting the raiders, and the farm fell free of them. All summer black-and-orange box-elder bugs climbed the stone steps to the back porch and pried their way through the door cracks to first take possession of the mud-room, then the kitchen, the parlor, and up the narrow steps to the trapped heat of the bedrooms. Once Esperance came back, belly full, and brushed the steps free of bugs. She started to push up the windows swollen tight in their frames, but the baby tugged at her back and pushed down so instead she settled for sitting in the closed parlor, drawing tiny breaths of musty air against the baby nudging up on her breastbone. Closing her eyes, she remembered the jar of mulberry jam she'd hidden in the cellar, tried to ignore the taste on her memory's tongue, smoothing the edges of the day. But it called to her just below the high raspy hum of the seven-year locusts, whose brown cases scaled the trunks of elms and oaks, then stopped suddenly and completely while their bodies broke free and their voices took possession of the limbs overhead.

She made a decision that afternoon, an act of will she had been unable to complete since the blue-eyed man rode into her yard. She would not descend the rough hand-split planks set at such a steep angle that she would have to lean back against the pull while she ran her fingers along the icy stone wall to the gap where she had tucked that one precious jar. She would leave it there, a sweet taste she would forego, a bargain she made for his life. Instead, she would go out to the potato patch and dig for the ruby ring her mother had buried when the Union soldiers had first come to their county. It was this ring, passed from her father's mother to her mother, that she dug and brushed clean and carried to barter the blue-eyed man's life free again, leaving her mother and sisters to their own devices in prison three counties away. The ruby was dull with dirt despite the pouch, but she shook it in her closed hand like a fly she'd caught, wanting to teach it a lesson before she turned it loose again. Esperance would never think her life amounted to much after that time, and gave her children the indifferent love she had left over.

It's a fine line between heaven and hell, my mother always said, and our family has always invented its own natural disasters. We build on river plains, then act surprised when our houses float downstream on the six o'clock news. The big bellied clouds lie around overhead filled with all our bad feelings. Romeo and Juliet were luckier than anyone in my family. They died before they had kids and ruined a bunch of lives. Shakespeare cheated us, only telling one side of the story, which always came out sad and lovely in a pathetic sort of way. But there's the rest of us, standing around like dumb cows beside the highway watching a car wreck twenty years in the making. As a kid, I always chose the losing side in games: the Confederate soldier, the captured wild horse, the Indian to everybody else's cowboy.

They called last night and said I had to come right away. Otherwise.

Tell Blu to come to the phone, I urged.

My parents spent fifty years in the locked room of their love. It's the privilege of poets to make such claims as my family does. Now I figure there's a dirt road between me and every place I want to go. I just can't stop sticking my toes in the flour-soft dust along the way. Blu will understand.

They had this tornado in Moberly and the roadsides are littered with animals. I've counted twenty raccoons, ten skunks, three dogs, five cats, seven deer, sixteen rabbits, a fox, twelve birds including a hawk whose wing still rises up, feathers ruffling as the semis go by. Everywhere I look there are fires and flood stains. The Grand River banks, raw with highway concrete and twisted trees. River-bottom fields, flat brown in the middle of summer as if they've been spewed with volcanic ash. You have to come as fast as you can, they said. Fly.

He needs you.

At the third gravel road I turn and begin to watch for the farm. It surprises me like always sitting on top of the hill instead of the bottom, the tall house with chimneys guarding either end, paint scalded off the boards, roof black and mossy, windows blasted out. Stalky mullein and primrose, Queen Anne's lace and milkweed, ragweed, and squirrel grass crowd the ruts of the driveway beyond the locked gate. Cattle collect under the box-elders and mulberries, more in the shade of the oaks and elms set off to the side there. Esperance is buried in the little cemetery further back, where the fence is falling down. I can see it from here. I should get out and fix it. Shoo the cattle away. Their hooves pack the ground, and the dust puffs up when they stomp flies.

It was just such a day I met Romulus Blue. Blu, he said, spelling it. That's what they call me. He'd just gotten back from road-racing school in California to improve his performance. He was fine on the short tracks. At the time I had no idea what he meant. Fifty years, my parents, in thrall to their desire. It took me fifteen minutes at the laundromat, watching him clumsily fold his T-shirts. His big hands with black dirt in the pores and creases. The one lazy eye that looked both ways when he turned his head. The big nose and the patch of hair on his chin, the beard he would try to grow three years running.

When he hit the wall it broke the brake rotor.

The ladder gave it away. My parents yelled, but I just kept going. Sneaking on past everyone up late or asleep. People in our little Iowa town would tell you they expected as much. Blu was waiting in his four-barrel rumbling against the August corn high as our heads on either side of the road. You can't stop love like that.

He never got more than a few scratches and bumps racing. Well, once knocked out for a day, but he came back fine. That one eye wandering off on its own when he looked at me, like it was trying see over my shoulder, around my body, catch a glimpse of what else was coming.

Knocked the fuel pump off, spilled the fuel. Then it ignited. He didn't realize the car was trailing fire all the way down the track. First they tried water, that just squirted the flames around, then they finally got the chemical pumper working. Some munged-up deal with the pressure.

I ask because the caller doesn't say. Is Blu alright?

You need to come now.

Is he going to be okay?

I've waited as long as I could, but I'm still too close, only twenty-five miles away. I turn off the engine and close my eyes for a minute, listening to the distant cawing of a crow in the top of the elm up the driveway while the afternoon heat buzzes around the car slowly ticking down. If I could stop now—

I touch the swelling of my stomach which just this month has reached the steering wheel's soft nudge. My grandmother went off with a man from Iowa whose father had served in the Union army stationed in Missouri. Half the family quit speaking to her

that day, and later when her son showed up with a federal mar-
shall's badge to arrest Uncle Whit, the other half stopped. Mama
used to sneak me back here when she fought with Daddy. Like
two teenagers, we'd speed along the country roads at night, eating chips and drinking coke in bottles we threw out the window.
The trip never seemed to take any time at all. Now I feel like I
had to walk across the country of February to get here.

Hurry. Just hurry.

You have to dream your way back to beginnings, that's why
stories start in the middle, like a lake fingering away from some
rock you can't see but imagine has to be there. Everything lives
in a bowl the size it requires. The bucket of night that holds our
melting sleep. Even the clay hard soil of Esperance's farm found
ways to use the burnt sticky liquor spilling from dreams. I know
Blu's gone on ahead of me now, so I stop in Missouri.

Dwight Tuggle

Dwight's neck hasn't been the same since Shelly Anderson turned a 336-MPH in her top-fuel dragster and his ex-wife called a 51-50 on him. Police hold for crazies. What was she thinking? He trims the gas on the mower and sets the choke so it roars along loud enough to wake the dead neighbors. They must be dead, otherwise he'd see them come out of the house. Their trash cans and recycling appear magically at the curb opposite his by the time he's pulling in his driveway from work at the welding shop each Wednesday evening, and by the time he's home the next evening, the empty containers have vanished. This is the only evidence that someone is in there. But even though the neighbors are invisible, when he looks across the street at their perfect green lawn, it's alive with activity.

A 500-year-old man pulls up in his twenty-year-old truck with his crew of alcoholics to mow there, as they do once a week. Dwight watches while the old man gets dragged to his knees by a tall seedling from one of the maple trees the city has planted up and down the block. Next thing he's trying to yank it out of the ground while one of the alcoholics steadies him back on his feet. It's the youngest one with long blond Kato Kaelin hair and surfer tan who helps him most times. The kid has the ruined, missing teeth of someone who spends too much time fighting in bars, although Dwight has never seen him uptown. The other, older

Jonis Agee

alkies stagger around behind the mowers like they're being pulled a little faster than their feet can manage. With the seedling dangling from his hand the old man yells at them. They've hit the young tulip tree in front there so many times it's dying. Maybe the neighbors will come out of the house when it does.

Last week Dwight asked the 500-year-old man about working with those boys.

"Wheelbarrows," he said.

"How's that?" Dwight said.

"Got to push 'em to get anywheres," the old man grinned, waiting for Dwight's laugh. He obliged. He wasn't the kind to hold out against another man's humor.

Dwight twists his neck to the left, waits for the pop, then to the right for the same effect. He has to do this about every half hour or the sonofabitch tightens up on him. He should sue that police department, sure as shooting they munged it up. His dry eyes sting and he squeezes them tight for a minute. Then he lets the mower lead him across the front which he does every four days now that he's had the Heavenly Acres people his cousin works for come and spray for white grubs and weeds while they fertilize. That yellow patch by the sidewalk is beginning to tint green again and the pachysandra circling the three-story fir is putting out new sprouts over the tire tracks. That fir is the biggest tree around. The neighborhood is mostly tidy, one-story houses with small uniform lots big enough for a detached garage to be stuck back there to one side. About half of the owners have poured concrete drives while the others, like Dwight, try to keep their gravel or crushed rock neat and weed-free. Every spring the lady next door comes along and plants the bare circles along their block with giant marigolds in that bright highway-marker orange shade Dwight has never cared for, though it does make the street nicer, he has to admit.

"Handclippers, use the handclippers," the old man yells at the fat alkie whose belly hangs down like a giant unripe pumpkin where his T-shirt and pants part company. Even from here Dwight can see the greasy sweat clinging to his face and arms, darkening the gray T-shirt in big uneven patches as he sets the weed whacker down and picks up the clippers. The leaves on another branch of the tulip tree browned this past week. Sissy trees, Dwight decides, can't take being knocked around by a mower.

Dwight cuts the back and forth pattern he prefers in the front lawn, taking his time to set the wheels of the mower into the groove just beyond the last one so he'll get a good even cut. He's seen the woman to his left mow her lawn different every time and now look at it—grass doesn't know which way to grow anymore. She isn't the one called the cops on him, though she had every right to that night. For that he's willing to cut her some slack about the lawn. Once or twice he's even let the mower lead him across their invisible boundary and cut her yard too, so the green stretches in nice continuous stripes that he can enjoy out his picture window, where he sits of an evening, drinking cheap sweet wine and watching the activity up and down the street.

"You're just lonely," his ex said when she came to get him released from county lockup that time.

"I am not," he declared with the most absolute tone he could muster. He'd rather be crazy than lonely, he decided when she left the last time. He'd seen how loneliness made men seedy. He could pick them out a mile away. Being with a woman kept your pants pressed and your shirt cuffs ungreasy. You shaved and brushed your teeth. He skirts the pachysandra in one careful swipe and turns off the engine. As soon as the noise dies, he hears them across the street again, the kid with the blower strapped to his bare back walking up and down the walk while the old man instructs the fat alkie how to dig a hole.

Dwight wheels the mower over the gravel past his pickup into the garage where he has to squeeze by the GTO that caused most of the trouble, and looks at the end wall expecting to see the poster that caused the rest of the trouble, until he remembers that the neighbor lady has it. She wasn't the one went nuts that night, and he's been meaning to go over there for a week now, but hasn't got the nerve yet. He wants to explain and get the poster back if he can. Who knows, maybe she's a big fan too. His ex certainly isn't. He picks up a clump of grass that's fallen off the mower blade and retraces his path past the GTO's dusty white surface his shirt sleeve brushes, leaving a clear trail along the red racing stripe. He hasn't had the heart to come out and give it a good bath and polish since that night with the ex.

"It's not like I'm kidnapping the neighborhood children, Eloise," he'd yelled, and she got this odd expression like maybe she thought he was.

The men across the street load their equipment and disappear quickly, leaving the silence to recapture the neighborhood. The only kids left in the houses around him are teenagers who make their presence known like bats by appearing only at dusk, when they load themselves into their loud cars and rumble away to a heavy bass beat. Not one of them has ever asked Dwight about the GTO, but a couple of times he's seen what he thinks is envy in the eyes of the kid who belongs across the street when Dwight passes him on the way to give it a run and blow out the carburetor. It has its own deep rumble of growling power ready to spring, and Dwight has to be careful at stop signs not to press the gas down hard the way he has to on the truck.

"Have you ever, in your whole life I mean, ever raced a car, Dwight?" Eloise asked the night he bought the car from that kid from Ottumwa. She knew right where to hit a man. Oh, she went for the ride with him all right, but only to pick a fight. So he'd told her she couldn't drive it.

"This is too much car for you, honey. You'd wreck it before you got out of second gear." He hadn't meant it to be the woman fight again. Eloise always thinks he's saying what he's not. When he got the old poster of Shirley Muldouney with her funny car at the swap meet, he wasn't thinking of throwing it up at her either.

As he steps into the kitchen the phone rings and he quickly picks it up. It's the lady next door.

"Dwight," she says in that out of breath way that sounds like she's just run up from the basement and caught the ringing phone. But that's not what's confusing him, it's the first name business she's picked up since the police came that night. Like she knows him better now that she's seen his head locked under that blue arm.

"Yeah." He's feeling cautious and rubs at his left eye which is tearing again though the doctor said using the drops would help.

"Saw you mowing," she says.

"Uh huh." The eye stings and itches so he rubs it some more.

"You there for a minute? I have something for you."

"Yeah." He turns on the water and scoops some up to his eye.

"I'll be right over," she warns and hangs up.

"Fine," he mutters into the dead receiver before he hangs it up.

His eye is burning now and he holds the hand towel hard against it, trying not to rub. "Dry Eye," the doctor called it. Not allergies like his ex had insisted. Another case of her being better than stupid. There are two kinds of tears, the doctor had explained. Those that constantly lubricate the eye and those that are produced as a response to irritation or emotion. "You need both." The doctor had tried to enforce some kind of will here, Dwight felt, as if he were the source of his own trouble. But the pamphlet had explained it as a failure of the meibomian glands to produce enough oily layer to smooth the tear surface and reduce the evaporation of tears. He puts the towel down and looks at the little bottle of artificial tears sitting on the counter next to the sink. This happened mostly to women in menopause, the doctor had told him. Or especially people using pain relievers, sleeping pills, medication for nerves, diuretics, antihistamines, or alcohol. The doctor'd paused at alcohol like he'd been uptown recently himself, but Dwight had stared right back at him, refusing to blink.

When the knock rattles the aluminum screen door in back, Dwight pushes the bottle of tears back behind the copper-toned canister set. "Yeah," he calls.

"Got some coffee?" The compact figure edges past him toward the kitchen holding something wrapped in a red-and-blue plaid cloth napkin. "Hot," she explains as she sets it down on the gray

Formica table with the thick aluminum legs Eloise traded him for the little maple kitchen set right after she left. He'd been in that accommodating mood then, hoping she'd see the better side of him and come back. Lot he knew.

"In the maker—" He waves to the Mr. Coffee he keeps going all day even when it's too warm out for anything but iced tea. He likes the smell of coffee just on the verge of burning, it reminds him of the bad old days with Eloise, a kind of balance for all that nostalgia business that keeps threatening to drive him down the road. He doesn't drink but a cup a day himself. Caffeine can make a man's hands jumpy, he explained more than once, but she kept it brewing like he might someday relent and go on the kind of binge some of those guys uptown indulged in every weekend with their beer.

"Cup?" She stands with her hand resting on the handle of an open cabinet door.

Dwight reaches over her head and pulls one out. She's a lot shorter than Eloise, and squarer, he notices. Built like a bale of straw. Few curves.

"Aren't you having anything?" she asks as she fills her cup. "Might need something to wash this down." She whips the cover off the Pyrex dish and the aroma of coffee cake escapes. "Walnut cinnamon," she says. "Some plates would be good, and a knife and some butter." She laughs. "Sorry—guess I should've had you to my place."

When they are settled at the table, plates of hot cake steaming in front of them, Dwight takes a bite and feels a hot walnut lodge like a bullet, pressing on the nerve where the temporary crown has worn off his left upper molar. He turns his head away and tries to move it with his index finger, pretending he's looking out the window over the sink toward the dead people's house. Eleven A.M. on a Saturday morning and still no sign of life.

"Coffee's nice and strong," she says.

He nods.

"So—"

He nods again as if she's said something, then remembers how this used to drive Eloise crazy. "Good, it's pretty good." He takes another bite and chews on the right side. It isn't bad. He takes a sip from the glass of water he's gotten to make her feel comfortable. She smiles and chews so he smiles back. She isn't bad-looking. Brown hair, brown eyes, straight nose, round face. He usually goes for the blondes, but brown is okay too. Most blondes are dyed anyway, he realized after living with Eloise and smelling that peroxide every month that chewed its way through a person's sinuses. Probably gave him Dry Eye. He'll tell her that next time he sees her.

She's a healthy eater, he notices as she cuts another piece while she's still swallowing the first one. She holds the knife over the cake and raises her eyebrows at him but he shakes his head.

"Sorry about the butter. Saturday's my shopping day," he says.

She picks at a large crumb on her plate, placing it on the tip of her tongue that rolls out ever so slightly like the lizard's he saw last night on TV. "Where do you shop, Dwayne?"

"Dwight."

"Dwight," she grins. "Sorry. I'm terrible about names. I'm Bonnie."

"I shop at Larry's Food King. That way I can take the GTO out for a spin. Go all the way around the long route." His eye is stinging and he can feel the stringy mucus crusting at the edges, but he doesn't want to dab at it and draw attention. He swallows and flexes his thick fingers to make sure he isn't getting that dry mouth and arthritis which would mean he has Sjögren's Syndrome, for which they have both a foundation and a national association. Sometimes he wishes the doctor would keep his pamphlets to himself. Right after Eloise left he spent a month of panicky nights worrying about prostate cancer after he read the stuff in the waiting room. "You're fine," the doctor told him later, "still too young to worry about that one." Those lonely nights of worry made him aware as nothing else had how much he was going to miss his wife. That's when he started trying to get her back, surprising them both.

"I like that GTO," Bonnie says.

"Everybody except my ex-wife likes that GTO."

Bonnie cocks her head, appraising him like a piece of swap meet goods. "Maybe that's why she's your ex."

Dwight feels his face flush and his eye tear furiously, and suddenly he hopes she doesn't think he has a bar tan. Since that drunken night with the police, Eloise has barely spoken to him. He shrugs.

"Guess I have to be honest," Bonnie says. "I was hoping I could get a ride with you to the store. My car's on the fritz and I'm stuck for the weekend. My mechanic's that guy with the '87 Corvette you saw the other night?" She uses her little fingernail to clear the small gap between her front teeth.

Dwight remembers the Corvette because it was Eloise driving it. A loaner, she called it, but he knew better. Bad enough he'd had a few uptown before he drove home and found the yellow-and-black Corvette sitting in the driveway. Then he'd gone back to the garage and she was rummaging through his tools for something, he never did find out what. Just the sight of her sitting on the hood of the GTO, possibly causing a dent with her little heart-shaped butt, made him go nuts. The poster of Shirley Muldouney staring down at their fight, that crooked smile on her face like a smirk. She could afford to look that way, she'd survived her crash when the car-flipping blow over came. That was one thing he didn't want to see again, that damn poster. He'd torn it off the wall while Eloise accused him of everything under the sun, including wanting to sleep with Shirley Muldouney, a person he had wanted his wife to become and then not let her, so now she was going drag racing with Leo Farnam's Corvette. At least he was willing to teach her. To his credit, Dwight had not attacked the car. That would be wrong, that's for sure. Instead, he started ransacking his own house, tossing furniture and dishes out of windows while Eloise frantically dialed 911. Hearing the ruckus with the rest of the neighborhood, Bonnie had come over and rescued the poster and his Jim Force replica dragster from the heap Dwight was trying to set fire to as the two police cars pulled up onto the lawn on either side of the big fir tree, crushing the straggles of pachysandra. That had about made him truly crazy.

"Leo's got 600-horsepower in there now. With an automatic transmission. Road Rocket."

Dwight shakes his head, his stomach souring with the memory of Eloise roaring off while he watched out the back window of the squad car, his neck already kinking up good. "650 foot-pounds of torque with factory engine displacement. Twin turbos take time to spool up though." She is watching him closely, Dwight can feel her eyes making his body slow way way down.

"It's slow in the zero-to-sixty run then," he says looking out the window just in time to see the front door across the street open and the dead people straggle out blinking with hands held up to their brows against the sun.

"Sixty to 100 takes about eight seconds. Don't want to mess with it then, but before that—"

He glances at the little gap between her front teeth that is somehow more endearing now. "The GTO could take it," he says though he has no experience whatsoever. Eloise had been right about that.

Bonnie pushes back her chair and stands. "Let's go see."

And while Dwight has absolutely no idea why, doesn't know anything about this woman and her obsession with cars, he lets her lead the way out the back door, his eye tearing madly in the dry wind blowing across the neighborhood.

Mile a Mud

Nate is off running WW2 in the jeep division of the Swamp Buggy Races down at Naples when it all happens. Busts loose. Gram following Uncle Heat, her son, across the porch and right down those steps, holding that old kitchen knife her other son Star made her the summer before he disappeared. She says she knows Star is dead. In a dream he told her how he was on the levee road going to see that Ruth in Taberville when the fog come up and he knew he should've stopped but he kept on driving. She was already pregnant with Nate so he had to get there before she got off work at two A.M., or she'd have no faith at all in him. Long and short of it—off he goes and the river was high from a week of rain, though it's never low in that spot.

Every summer Gram takes a pot of birthday flowers to the place Star showed her by those two old black walnuts with the big slab of granite that was just like a diving board his truck must've bounced on and flung off into those muddy moccasin-bitten Florida waters. Well, not unlike the swamp water Nate races in three times a year. The first time they fill the track for the Winter Classic in March there are few critters, but by summer, like this time I am speaking of, that water is home to catfish, frogs, moccasins, and a couple of stray gators. The Muddy Mile, they call it.

"Don't you leave your foot or arm down there," I tell Nate.

He's saving for an air-cooled, v-8 buggy, like that one called Cause For Divorce, but I'm not saying anything when it comes to that. Nate has the lot of us to feed, and it's no secret a person needs the Lord's own rest once in a blue moon. He pulls the jeep to Naples behind the pickup he borrows from the garage. Can't even afford a trailer.

I'm half-distracted trying to catch Bonnie Jolly's race in the v-8s. Fatal Attraction, she calls her swamp buggy. She's driving dump trucks, raising horses and sixty foster kids, plus three of her own, the TV commentator says. I know what that's like, I think as Uncle Heat turns over one of Nate's new planters he's welded from pieces of cars those kids wreck weekends out on the interstate.

"It's not right," I tell him every time one of the planters shows up in the yard.

"Never you mind," he says and manages to sell it next time a car stops for honey or walnuts, berries or vegetables rotating the year around at the stand on the blacktop out front of our place.

Uncle Heat stops outside the window next to the TV and tries to argue that knife out of Gram's hand. They've been arguing since the day Star died, although Heat insists that Gram never liked him much before that either. Once or twice she's hinted that he was in that Ruth's bed too. With Star and Ruth both gone, Heat has no one to stand up for him. He's reaching for the knife now, but she's holding that knife pointed at him with the wood handle squarely against her little caved in belly that hangs down like a sad pink apron those nights I have to help her into her sleeping gown, usually after another set-to with Uncle Heat, who doesn't dare reach for that blade she takes her own self to the whetstone outside the tool shed. Sitting in the rusty iron tractor seat and peddling the stone like a four foot pie plate between her knees, she hones that blade sharp enough to cut the moon if she takes a mind she needs a piece of that too. Around and around that stone whirls, sparks jumping off where the blade touches, like crickets in the fry pan that time Uncle Heat dumped a whole sackful he collected for his lizards in her flour bin and she scooped out enough to coat her chicken with.

* * *

"What's at the bottom of that Sippi Hole?" I ask Nate the day before he leaves for Naples. I already know it's named for a man from Mississippi who always got stuck there on the track.

And Nate says, "China, maybe. You don't wanna know."

Then he gives me a one-armed hug, the kind where his thick fingers leave greasy prints on the side of my breast and I think on that till after supper dishes when the two of us slip off for the tool shed where he stores the ww2 jeep and the parts car. There's this mattress he keeps leaning up against the wall, covered with an old tarp so the birds won't mess it. We do this while the girls watch TV with Gram. Her hearing aid's turned off. She only pretends to laugh with the girls as she works against time to finish crocheting that bedspread she started for Star forty years ago.

Uncle Heat's in his room, the old summer kitchen off the back of the house, playing with those lizards and thinking up some new devilment for his mother. I dread every catalog and salesman comes along because of him. But he's had his share of trouble too. More than Star died that night he disappeared.

In the shed, Nate lays that mattress down on the tarp and takes the clean sheets out of the trunk of the parts car. We slide the bolt on the shed door and only keep that one twenty-watt yellow bug bulb going over the toolbench. Nights the moon is big and strong enough to march in through the window in pale white squares across the room at us, we don't need no light at all.

We take it all different ways. Tearing at each other like hogs rooting in the mud over at the neighbors, or gentle and coy as their milk cows batting their big brown eyes at the bull. It's the good between us, the way his hands get so clean touching me, so clean I take the oil stained fingers to my mouth and savor the burnt engine taste on my tongue.

I never liked a smoking man, but when Nate first kissed me, the tobacco recent on the tip of his tongue, I liked that too. Even when he smoked afterward and then we did it again, knocking the ashtray over, rolling in the ash, there was nothing could sully it for me.

Nate has this way of touching my nipples as if he understands from the calipers, the quarter turns, the small degrees of adjustment for his engines. I catch him when I open my eyes, his ear pressed to my stomach, listening for the perfect pitch my breathing makes as he squeezes my puckered nipple between those big flat fingers. He's a listening man. Behind us the vehicles sit in their protective silence like twin hearts between beats.

There is a ticking hush in the shed after our noise is through, and the taste of him in my mouth from the oily air. A sparrow in the rafters fluffs its wings and cheeps once and it sounds so downright lonely waiting up there for daylight. In the corner on the workbench, a mouse threads its way among the pop cans, bolts, and wrenches, a tiny trail of noise until the girls laugh extra loud and it carries itself all the way out to us like fresh water in a pail, and I wrap my leg over his thigh and let the sweat slide it off again.

"Nate," I whisper, "what if you tip over in that water and get trapped?"

He turns me away and pulls me against him, crossing his thick forearm over my chest, gradually pressing it up into my throat. "I'll be hung in the harness maybe, and drown—" He slowly cuts off my breath, and I let him. He'll stop in time. He's listening. I relax and imagine the muddy swamp water slipping into my mouth.

* * *

Nate smiles into the TV camera, good strong white teeth. He's won his round and can move on. Outside the window Uncle Heat is pulling up his shirt, offering Gram his apple-hard belly. She's accused him of running Star into the river in a fit of jealousy, and now she hesitates as if she's measuring the work ahead of her knife, the one Star carved a handle for from a piece of that black walnut Uncle Heat was making a bed out of. Star used one of the spokes meant for the foot board, and there's still a gap where it was supposed to go. When Heat offered it to her, Gram refused the bed, not because of the missing spoke, but because it was the same black walnut a storm dropped on her husband and killed him. Star came closer to understanding Gram by making a walnut knife she could use to hack a fresh chicken to pieces with or hold Uncle Heat in his place like now.

I see him reach for it and when she won't let go, his hand slips along the shaft, the blood falling from the blade in a sticky curtain.

"Uncle Heat!" I holler, knowing I'll miss Nate's race when I run out there. Gram throws the knife down as if finally recognizing its evil intent. Uncle Heat wraps his hand in her apron so she has to untie it and bind the strings around and around the red soaking cloth while Heat's eyes are so naked with gratefulness it reminds me of the way you hold a rabbit in your arms just before you break its neck with that little popping click.

They're announcing Nate's race, and I look in the window in time to see the jeeps floundering through the deep muddy water of the Sippi Hole, only the helmeted heads, roll bars, and exhaust stacks showing as one of them stalls in the wash back from the leaders.

"They're only thirty-two inches off the ground!" I yell.

I'm trying to sort out the colors, but Nate's green is too close to the muddy brown of the water now. Uncle Heat sits down abruptly, his bloody hand soaking shirt and pants. Gram's staring at him like he's put those lizards in her bathwater again as he closes his eyes and lets his long body unfold onto the ground.

"Oh Nate," I say and kneel down next to Uncle Heat who is surprisingly thin, almost frail in this position, like an exhausted boy asleep in his bed.

The TV crowd's yelling as the engines sputter and roar toward the checkered flag. If Nate hasn't used enough silicone, if water's in the engine, if the Sippi Hole's caught him—I'm listening for his name as I lean my face next to Uncle Heat's mouth, waiting for the moist sour breath that never seems to come—

"It's only a scratch," I say. "Get up now." But it's Nate I'm thinking of, Nate in the berry-red-stained shirt, gator-tumbled on his way to China or some darker waters without me.

By the time I get Uncle Heat up again—blood makes him faint —Gram's taken her knife back to the kitchen but agrees to stitch and bandage the hand if he sits still. The girls who've been over to the neighbors all day drag themselves inside with a baby king snake ringed red and yellow and white, bright as you please, which I make them take right back outside. There's enough of that with Heat—no sense letting it become a family thing.

Everyone's settled down good and I sneak off for the TV again, collapsing in my armchair just in time to see Nate and the Swamp Buggy Queen take a leap into the Sippi Hole together, bouncing up in each other's arms, grinning through the muddy waters streaming down their faces, over the black, spangled evening dress that stands up pretty well to the soaking, and there's no missing the puppy plump, eighteen-year-old upper arm Nate has his fingers around.

"Thought they only let the winner of the V-8 Stock division throw her in," I say to the TV. And for the first time today, I feel like Star, driving my life in a fog, just seconds away from disaster.

The Luck of Junior Strong

"Can't escape necessity," Uncle Marv announced as he propped the broom and dustpan in the corner where Junior could reach it and waved in the direction of the bathroom.

"I wouldn't think of it." Junior used the toe of the boot cast on his left leg to push the table far enough away so he could unjam the wheel that had caught and caused the mess to begin with. The walk-out basement of Marv's house was fixed up like a family room with a gas grate in the fireplace and a brown-and-yellow linoleum block floor in a shuffleboard pattern, though nobody remembered how to play the game. The bar was a red Naugahyde and rust dotted chrome affair with a dripping water faucet in the half-sink, a tiny built-in fridge that wouldn't freeze ice, and cloudy mirrors behind the empty shelves that held bottles of liquor until Marv quit drinking after the airplane crash coming home from the Iowa State/University of Iowa football game four years ago.

It was the black-and-gold foam Hawkeye headpiece that saved Marv, they said, when the other fellas in the small plane died at the site. Marv took up his life with greater seriousness after that, ignoring the national media and going to the philosophy and religion section of their town's little public library instead. A year later he discovered Buddhism and it had been downhill ever since. It had gotten so the family avoided him at holiday dinners unless they were armed with drinks and other people. He was their favorite person to sic on newcomers to the family. On the other hand, Marv was the only person who offered to take Junior in after the hospital released him.

"Well, this couch folds out just like this—" Marv reached behind the black leather back and pulled a lever and the front unfolded with an awkward sigh like a fat woman dropping her drawers. He straightened and looked at Junior in the wheelchair, his broken legs splayed in their heavy casts. "Maybe we should just leave it open."

"Long as I can get around it." Junior pushed the wheels forward to see if he could edge between the chrome barstools and the bed.

"No reason to go back there anyway." Marv tilted his head toward the knotty pine cabinets on the back wall in the corner that held games and puzzles.

"Okay, leave it then. I can get through the doorway for the bathroom and the patio this way." Junior backed the chair up and wheeled himself toward the unfinished part of the basement which held the toolbench, furnace, and concrete floored bathroom with the rust-stained sink and shower. He didn't know how he was supposed to take a shower, but he was too tired and pissed off to mention that fact.

"I'll be going pretty soon, so if you need anything—" Marv headed for the stairs. "Have to be there early tonight." He paused, his thick-fingered hand on the knotty pine door frame. He almost smiled and Junior knew he was supposed to show some interest.

"Why's that?"

"Teaching a new class—Guilt: Let it go, Let it go, Let it go." Marv smiled for real and Junior obliged with a shake of his head and a hand wave.

Marv had told him there'd be no Christmas here, not since he was a Buddhist now. And that he'd be gone every evening to the Center to meditate and give classes. He never got paid for these, but he acted like he did. During the day, he worked as packaging supervisor at the small bottling plant on the outskirts of town. Junior looked around at the various framed certificates and photos over the mantel. According to these, Marv had a college degree in packaging and was a certified Packaging Management Institute Graduate. Although he'd made a lot more money at his previous job with a big manufacturing firm in Cedar Rapids, Marv had quit to have more time to open the Center with two other Buddhists after the plane wreck and reading had taken him to this higher consciousness.

Before the crash, people used to say that Marv was the kind of guy who knew when to buy you a beer. After the crash, he'd acted pissed as hell until his birthday dinner four months later when his wife announced that he had webbed toes and she felt like she was in Jurassic Park every time he climbed in bed. After that she up and left him for good.

Later, when he first started in on the Buddhism, he'd say things like, "Did you ever see a hearse with a trailer hitch? You need celestial pull not tractor pull." That was when the relatives started acting shy.

While Marv was helping him get settled, Junior hadn't thought about food, but now his stomach grumbled as the light began to fail outside, sheeting the windows and glass patio doors with dark gray. As they drove back from the hospital in Iowa City where they'd airlifted him after the crash, the winter sky had worn that thick felt overcast all afternoon. Now it seemed to squat down, obliterating the huge old cottonwoods outlining the backyard, turning the icy snow flat and dull. The wind died and a silence took over that made him nervous and too alert. Even the crows that usually collected in the treetops squawking and flapping about this time of day failed to make an appearance.

Junior wheeled himself over to the phone on the fieldstone mantel and pulled the cord so it flopped down in his lap, banging his little finger against the chair arm. He still had enough pain-killer in him it didn't bother him that much though. He couldn't remember the number for pizza, but after wrangling with information, he captured it and called. Lucky he had had some cash when Marv showed up at the hospital to take him home. No telling when he'd get to a bank. Actually, the money wasn't technically his. Not yet at least. Well, maybe. Junior tried to brush the facts aside, as he'd done for the past week lying in bed after they'd operated on his legs and feet, putting the screws and plates in and keeping him on a nice float of drugs.

"You're lucky," they said, but he figured they told everyone that. What did they know about cars and racing, especially about hoping to make it as a driver with two bum legs? One turn around the track when he was supposed to be taking the damn car to the other garage with the cash in his pocket to pay for the blower they were going to install. He didn't think it would matter, he'd done it before, snuck a car out for a quick turn around the track so he could practice.

"Levon?" The yellow and red pizza box came down the stairs followed by a pair of jean clad legs and finally the shoulders and blonde head of a girl. In the odd lighting, he couldn't see who it was at first, not until she put the pizza on the bar and unzipped her black ski jacket.

"Sharee—" he said, reaching for the dollars stacked on the bed beside his chair.

"My dad said it was you who called, so I figured I'd come over and see how you're doing." She pulled her jacket off and slung it over the bar.

"So how ya doing?" Her frank blue eyes made him want to lie, to make her look beyond what he appeared like at this moment.

"Had some luck, I guess. I'm okay, how about you?"

She smiled, keeping her lips pressed together, and sat down on the bed. That's when he remembered why he'd only gone out with her a couple of times, long enough to get her to sleep with him, then stopped. She never talked. Almost never. Great, the one person comes to visit him besides his crazy uncle is a mute girl who called him by his old high school name, Levon. A name he'd changed to Junior for his budding career in racing.

"How's that pizza?" He nodded toward the box and she jumped up and brought it over, placing it on the bed next to his chair.
Flipping the lid, she looked at him and smiled again, teeth carefully
covered. He remembered those buck teeth that made her look like
a rabbit with a cause. The top of the pizza was coated with a jum-
ble of colors and shapes of items he hadn't ordered. "What's this?"

"I told Dad to make it special." She blushed and picked at the
fuzzy balls on the faded pink blanket covering the foldout mattress.

He pried a piece up and took a big dripping bite. "Not bad.
You want some?"

She shook her head.

When he'd demolished half the pizza, he folded the lid down
and leaned back and closed his eyes wishing for something to
drink. He was really really thirsty, the way he'd been the whole
time since the accident. The pain medication, they told him.

"Think you could get me a glass of water?" he asked without
opening his eyes. He heard her get up and leave the room. A
minute later she was back, the glass dripping on his hand.

* * *

Sharee showed up every day for two weeks bringing him pizza and
buffalo wings and cheese breadsticks from her dad's place until he
was getting pretty sick of it, even Christmas Eve and Day when his
uncle was meditating for twenty hours straight. Marv was too
busy to cast more than an occasional thought toward Junior's well-
being, so if it weren't for Sharee he'd probably starve, he figured,
even though he rarely got more than a couple of words out of her.
Maybe she was studying with Marv, he joked to himself in the
long afternoons watching the red squirrels chase each other up one
dark green clothes pole, along the wire, then down the other, over
and over.

He spent a lot of his time reading and watching the weather out
the back windows. Marv subscribed to several newspapers and

magazines although he never seemed to have time to do more than leaf through them and grunt or let out a hoot at something dumb another person was doing with their life. Junior tried watching television but with racing in rerun, he was left with talk shows. Jenny Jones reminded him of some of his high school teachers, dressed a little out of style and full of mocking opinions usually only mothers could agree with. He imagined his mother in the living room of her little farmhouse seventy-five miles away cheering Jenny Jones for her good sense, while he only felt depressed by the constant parade of people with incredibly bad judgment. When the strippers came on and needed makeovers just to grocery shop, it seemed so obvious that they were just cheap, low-rent girls with no taste.

As the painkillers slowly ran out and he began to feel the first stabs of healing, he began to identify with Montel. Montel was serious trouble. No smirking or giggling at these people. Montel stood up and told it like it was. Montel was the man. "Look right in that camera there," he instructed one guest. "I want all the women in your town to know what a dirty, lying dog you are. I want them to see you coming so we don't have to have you on another show like this one." Junior agreed one hundred percent.

Sitting in Marv's basement watching talk shows and waiting for his legs to heal so he could get his racing career started, Junior was beginning to take on more of a global perspective. He needed evidence of something, luck maybe, that's what he told himself anyway. He had a whole shirt box full of clippings from around the world, and not one of them was from the *National Enquirer.* After the movie *Anaconda,* he found a report that an eighteen-foot serpent had killed three little kids in the Peruvian jungle by toppling their fishing boat and crushing them. In another story, forty-three people were devoured by piranha when the bus carrying them along rain flooded roads to vote in local elections fell into a river in the Amazon. Not all the stories were this drastic, but they did share some element of surprise that had surprised him. Like the man who held up a coffee shop with a live goose that he threatened to strangle, if someone didn't produce some cash. Three people ran for the ATM!

When Sharee came clumping down the stairs carrying a plastic box of salad and some slightly stale garlic bread, he had today's story ready to share. The lettuce was a little discouraged looking, the edges trimmed in brown and the tomatoes turning that peculiar deep mealy rose, but he dutifully squirted the tube of Caesar dressing out and ate as quickly as he could. The only thing fresh she'd brought was a bottle of Mountain Dew, his favorite since she told him he looked like one of the guys in the ad leaping out of the airplane on a snowboard. She'd glanced at his casts and got embarrassed then, but he hadn't taken offense.

"Sharee," he said after he'd finished eating. They were propped up on the sofa bed, side by side, fully clothed. It didn't even scare him. He could feel the first surge of caffeine from the Dew and it made him like her more. He leaned over and kissed her lips, trying not to press too hard since he'd discovered the braces she now wore over those rabbit teeth. So far she hadn't been willing to open her mouth to him, but he figured it was only a matter of time. Anything can be done in time, he was learning. Montel spent a lot of his shows trying to convince weak people of this fact while Jenny just seemed to laugh at them. That's the difference he had tried to explain to Marv late one night as they watched a rerun of Jenny after Jay Leno was done. Marv almost never stayed up to watch TV and almost never did more than poke his head down the stairs to check on Junior once or twice a day, sometimes now only hollering from the top of the stairs. It made Junior appreciate Sharee all the more. He was taking his time with her, trying not to scare her off. He would put his arm around her and let his fingertips rest right on the side of her breast. He never moved them up to the nipple, but he would glance down and see it harden at his nearness. He tried to remember what it had been like that time before, but since the accident, his earlier life seemed to have happened to someone else maybe, because he sure didn't feel like those were things he'd think or do.

"Sharee." He pulled away and picked up the latest clipping he had for her. She quickly covered her mouth with her hand, but he could tell from the shining in her eyes that she was eager to hear what he had to tell her. In fact, her eyes were a particularly nice blue today, like the January sky out there in the backyard, high and blue, so blue you knew it had to be cold because any heat would take away some of the shimmer. A blue-eyed blonde—he'd slept with her the first time to find out if she was a real blonde. That's what he'd wanted to brag. But he hadn't told anyone because, truth be told, Junior had to admit that he really didn't have any friends. He knew guys at the garage, at the track, men he worked with, but he didn't go to their houses, meet their wives or girlfriends. And it hadn't mattered much until these past few weeks sitting around waiting for someone to show up, send flowers or cards. Only people he'd heard from were the insurance agents for the track, the car owner, and the garage. They were all trying to figure out what to do with him. He could sympathize—he was trying to figure out the same thing.

"Levon," Sharee surprised him.

"Yeah?" He had the clipping right in his hand, the one about John Livermore who started a gold rush in Nevada, one of five major gold discoveries he'd made in his life. "The Babe Ruth of Gold Mining." The picture of Livermore showed a sly man who kept everything to himself as he looked up at the camera, that Sharee-like smile on his thin lips. Levon wasn't sure why he wanted to give this story to her, but it had to do with luck. Maybe something he was trying to explain to her about his future, but not in so many words. Bad luck for the prospector who lived in a shack and panned for gold until his death. Bad luck for the "trespassers" who were thrown off the property after Livermore showed up with his bulldozer. Livermore's good luck seemed to cost everybody else something.

"Come on." She stood up and pulled the wheelchair close so he could climb in. Then she went to the furnace room for his coat. The past few days she'd insisted they go out on the patio while the sun was bright even though it was freezing ass cold. He'd done it because it was easier than hassling with her about it.

But once outside, Sharee started pushing his chair off the patio and around the corner of the house, up the little hill where he worried they'd slip on the icy snow, and finally to the pizza van in the driveway. "We're going for a ride." She opened the door and started lifting under his arms until he waved her off and bracing himself half-hopped, half-climbed up onto the seat, pulling his bum legs in after him with his hands.

It was okay riding along although he found his feet seeking brake pedals and his hands reaching to brace against the dash of the van more than he liked. It wasn't even that Sharee was a bad driver. Maybe the empty boxes and cans sloshing around behind them made him nervous, he decided, but he couldn't ignore the way the other cars seemed to leap out of the distance at him, and the poles and fences, especially the stone walls, seemed to cut too close to the van.

That day in the car, he'd wound it up to the top in every gear, stretching her, feeling the nose tug at the white line, the rear end threatening to skip out with every shift. At 150 MPH, the G-forces began to push him away from the wheel, trying to pull him out the far side window, and he had to fight his body until his elbows ached with the struggle and his eyes teared. At 180 he thought his neck was going to come apart, and his ears suddenly plugged with a fierce ringing. His lungs felt smaller too, like the palm of a hand was pressing down too hard and he couldn't catch enough air. Still he hung on out of the third corner and bumped it up to 190, and that's when the engine let go and the rear end got loose and he took the wall. That's what he told them. "You're lucky," they said as they cut the car apart to get him out. Crying silently from the shattered bones, he could tell they were really pissed about the car.

Sharee took the turn onto the dirt road a little fast, sliding him toward her, then back against the door. "Sorry," she murmured and picked up the dark glasses off the dash and put them on. She had a nice profile, he noticed. A chin that didn't go too far in any one direction. In cars, she'd be something not too fast, good enough to learn on. Hit the low divisions where speed and cost were still under control before making the big time with Winston Cup. Maybe Busch Grand National but not quite. She sneezed and rubbed the bottom of her nose with her hand. "Dust—" she said.

The dirt road was bare and rose behind them in dusty clouds that drifted up and across the fields on either side, coating the snow tan. This was a frontage road that ran parallel to the interstate visible between the dips and rises of farmland. He hadn't been along here in years, if ever. He couldn't remember. What was it Uncle Marv said this morning? Something about needing to remember to discover and to discover to remember. The man was an almanac of bad philosophy, about as accurate as that one the farmers around here used for the weather. Look at today—perfectly good out there when the whole week was supposed to be clobbered with storms and arctic winds.

"We're here." Sharee nosed the van up to the wire gate with the For Sale sign on it, threw her sunglasses back on the dash as she got out, and played with the lock until it swung open. The sign overhead said Pleasure Island and in the distance beyond the acres of buckled asphalt parking lot, Levon could see the towers, loops, and hoops of an amusement park. Driving slowly over the humps and holes of the parking lot, Sharee nudged between the sand filled orange plastic pylons and wove around the Twister water slide, the Black Hole, and the Lazy River, all stranded and empty forms that showed themselves to be pathetic blue plastic and cheap metal constructions, fragile enough to be blown over by a good wind. They paused in front of a huge stack of inner tubes, apparently for the Lazy River, which were now glazed with ice and handfuls of snow caught in the crevices. The top of the stack was splattered with white clumps and streams of bird shit. Next to the inner tubes, along the fence for keeping nonpaying people out of the water rides, were a row of peeling kayaks standing on their ends, some ten or twelve slowly deflating bumper boats, a slew of paddleboats, and some water cannons. All bore similar marks of bird occupation, and when he looked at the ground, he could see the large prints of crows circling the piles as if they were inspecting the goods for auction.

Driving around the grounds, they found long rows of octagonal picnic tables, chaise lounges, table umbrellas, lawn mowers, and tools behind the several locked white metal utility sheds, which sat at some distance from the main one-story building that was really a long pole barn with lots of windows and the front cut out for easy access to the booths of food, drinks, and souvenirs. On the far side of the building, next to the merry-go-round, ferris wheel, roller coaster, and tilt-a-whirl, rested a thirty-foot parade float with last summer's crepe paper flowers bleeding black and gold, the Hawkeye colors, and still bright neon blue onto the snow. The chicken wire shape of the giant bird on skis, one wing flung into the air while the other attached itself to what was probably a tow rope of flowers from the tiny boat plowing through chicken wire water, seemed to wave directly at them.

"Come on." Sharee parked beside the float and was out the door before he could say anything. By the time she had his chair assembled and waiting, he had resigned himself. After a series of awkward and painful maneuvers they were seated side by side on a long bench sealed inside the driver's compartment. It was dry, almost cozy with the hot sunlight coming through the scratched plexiglass windshield positioned between the legs of the hawk.

"Here we go," she said and peeled off her down ski jacket which she shoved into the corner behind him before tugging at his jacket. He submitted since he was already beginning to feel too warm. His legs ached pretty good from all the moving around, and he wanted to keep the rest of his body as comfortable as possible. Marv's advice for dealing with pain. "The mind is the last faculty to submit," he'd added last night when Levon complained about the casts getting wet when he tried to bathe by lying down on the moldy concrete floor, half-in, half-out of the shower stall.

"What do you think?" She smiled, letting the corners of her lips spread wide enough to show her braces without clamping her hand over them for the first time. "Neat, huh?"

He looked out the window and at the plywood ceiling and the dashboard with nothing but an ignition and steering wheel with a two slot shifter on the column in front of her. Made sense, you only needed one or two gears for a parade. "Nice—"

They both laughed and she slid forward so he was forced to lean back into the corner to give her more room. She lifted his left, then his right leg up onto the bench and squirmed around so she was kneeling on the floor beside him, with her hands on his thigh.

"My dad's maybe gonna buy this place." She rested her cheek on her hands, her yellow hair spilling across his knees in such a way that the sun caught and burnished it with a sudden gesture that made his hand reach and without intending to begin to stroke her head.

"Sharee—"

"Shhh—" She raised herself and pulled his head down until their mouths met, her lips drawn back while his lips caught the metal wires and cut themselves. As the first salty blood seeped into his mouth, the shrill alarm rose up his legs, spread across his stomach, numbing his chest and shoulders till his arms turned leaden, just like that afternoon at the track when he'd seen the needle climbing toward 200 MPH and panicked, letting go of the steering wheel. And now with Sharee holding his face tight against hers and the taste of his own blood on his tongue, Junior began to feel a weight tugging at his soul, a weight that said it was skill and luck that helped you find the line on the track, that tucked you safely into the groove where suddenly anything was possible.

Adjusting the Bite

I'm sorry, I always go with men with bad teeth, I want to tell my daughter, who is sobbing long distance at 1:30 in the morning. I want to explain how her father came into my life and after that Verne and Ernie and Stan and the others. Bad teeth. Really bad teeth. One time, I want to tell her accusing tears, I went with a man who only had four teeth left in his whole head. After a couple of weeks, even those were pulled. It wasn't so bad, someone gumming your tongue when they kissed you, nothing like you'd expect. After we broke up, he got fitted for the full set and ended up with a rich widow. You see how things work out, I could offer her, but instead I keep murmuring no, no, to her long list of sorrows.

She's right though. About her father. Bad teeth wasn't the only thing he had to offer. Nor was it the only thing I held against him at the end. I remind her of his failings, trying to equalize things, trying to take the sting out of his words. He drinks too much, smokes too much dope, really, he's a drug addict, you can't expect anything out of a person like that. But I'd had it, and now it was only natural that she would too. He waits until she is happy with her life, until she decides it's safe to ask for something finally because everything is going so grand, then he does it. Teaching lessons, he calls it. Lessons.

It's 2:00 A.M. when the first crash occurs. Her crying has risen from the deep wrenching sobs to the lighter, sniffing hiccups that let me talk, when there is a noise that sounds like a car scraping itself alongside the house, a tangle of whining sheet metal and splintering wood. Hold on, wait, don't hang up, I call to her as I fling the phone on the carpet and run to the porch door at the end of my bedroom. Don't hang up, please, I call and manage at last to get the rusty key turned in the lock. Outside the freezing rain falls like clear jelly, clinging to the trees and houses in drips that pull everything earthward. But there are no crashed cars, nothing except the click click of the ice as the wind pushes the limbs against each other and bits bump against the windows of the house. I almost forget to go back to the phone. No, that's not exactly right. It's that I don't want to go back to the phone, back to the story of what her father has done.

For years, I have kept his betrayals small, made him a minor character in our lives. When our talking turned into friendship, just two gal pals having it down, having it all down about those men, it was all I could do to keep my teeth locked around that memory buried deep deep within the throat of the past. It is a luxury now to stand with my back to the room, the phone on the floor, her cries rising like tiny bubbles to the surface of a glass of water I can leave on the table beside my bed. It is the way I slept after he lost his front teeth in a fight when he tried to sneak into the pit area at Bristol Motor Speedway. He'd hitchhiked all the way from Omaha to Bristol, Tennessee. Why not Indianapolis? I asked him. It's closer and more famous, for chrissakes. He looked at me with the dark empty spaces in his teeth like missing tiles at the Cloudview Drive-in theater outside town where we used to go and make out, as if it was so obvious now what I would never understand, he couldn't waste his time on me anymore.

There's moments like that, where you can see your future and your past in that single breath-held second, like the arm drawn back and already arcing toward you for the fist slamming in your face. Not that he ever hit me. Well, that one time. After that I learned to defend myself. Now, when the plate gets passed in a group of women, all I can contribute is that one time I let a man with missing teeth hit me. But I've never told my daughter this either.

I pick up the phone.

Who's there, she demands.

No one, I tell her.

Then who were you talking to, she asks.

You, I tell her, only you.

You said hang on, she says.

I meant you, honey, I meant don't go away, I say and she laughs for the first time. You know your father, I begin, and her crying words come in a breathless rush. The wind outside shifts and the lights in the room dim brown. Oh no, I say, wait. The power comes back up, and I look around me trying to memorize how the vacuum cleaner blocks the doorway where I left it two weeks ago when I ran out of commitment. My dirty clothes, boots, and shoes slather the space between the bed and vacuum cleaner, but I am afraid to kick anything out of the way. If the lights go, though, I will either be trapped here or have to negotiate my debris. I haven't lived like this since those early years with her father gone racing when I would wait to clean until he got home. Once he showed up in the middle of the night, scratched and tumbled, weeds sticking to his clothes. He'd hopped a freight from the Michigan Speedway down through Chicago, across Iowa, and had to jump off after it'd picked up speed outside town. I thought it was going to slow down, he lisped through the gap. He'd stored the fake teeth in his pocket just in case.

I want to tell her about that time, how I looked at him and realized that he had desires I knew nothing about, nothing. Still, we made love as always, in the twin beds with the legs roped together, while she slept in the other room, unaware that this man who leaped from moving trains, flailing through emptiness with his teeth tucked in a pants pocket, was a father who over the years would fail her again and again and again. How can you not call or write her? I'd ask him down the road. How can you be a week late picking her up? How can you send her a picture of a rotted cow carcass for her sixteenth birthday? How can you not fill in any of the missing parts of her life?

Outside there is a terrific crack, like gunfire breaking through the lines in a war that had been waged secretly until this moment, when my daughter's wails break forth, either freeing something or driving it mad at last. I rush to the window, separating the wooden slats of the blinds but can see nothing. There is another noise, from behind the house, as if I am being surrounded, about to be taken in battle. Wait, I tell her, something's happening. Out back, the ground and fence and trees are much too shiny in the lights, but my truck is safe. It's the ice, I realize, the trees, the world beginning to go down. I come back and tell her, about the ice, not about her father. Of him, I only repeat, he's an idiot, really, but the old clown I made him into for years is beginning to disappear, replaced by a person I have kept hidden so well, I thought he could never touch her. Never raise the fist of discovery as he has tonight.

I shouldn't even be here, she whispers, I wasn't meant to be alive.

No, no, I soothe, that's not so, you were meant to be here, that's why you are. But she knows the truth, because he has told her that too. His gift when she was twenty-one, the story of how I got pregnant and we tried to get an abortion but it was illegal then. Why didn't you get the abortion, she asked the day he told her, why didn't you? There was a final, hopeless criticism in her voice that made me feel weak, wobbly legged.

There's this ice storm, I tell her. It's been going on for hours and now the trees are beginning to break under the weight.

There's a blizzard here, she says, her voice clearing up as if once again her world is worse off than mine. She isn't blaming me for her father exactly, you see, but she isn't letting me off the hook.

I'm sorry, I tell her, really. I didn't know any better, I say, but now that she is an age I was not so long ago, with her own life rocking her, my excuses are wind driven husks of what were once full, vital, stalky reasons. She can't know that though. How the ice is building up even as we talk and sleep.

He's mean, she says and starts to sob again. He's just so mean.

No, I tell her, don't cry again. He's stupid, he's never made anything of his life except changing tires on racecars. Don't listen, I urge her. And I mean don't listen, please don't listen. Let him remain the village idiot, that minor fool of a deity in tribal religions. Don't elevate him, don't.

There are more cracks and booms along the street, but when I pull the wooden slats apart and peek out again, I see only the silver slanting rain attaching solid wherever it lands. Everything glitters at me, like knives with eyes, saying stay away, saying you can't get away, saying you can't keep us away.

He'd gone to Darlington, finally getting to travel with a crew breaking in their first racecar. It was March and storming like tonight. Omaha, we get ice this time of year. You'd think we'd get used to it. Like the other, you'd think we'd get used to it, wouldn't you? That's what I should say to her. But she doesn't know, does she? How the phone call came and I answered it thinking he was calling. Thinking he'd tell how they got the car qualified or didn't, how it was loose or tight, how they kept having to adjust the bite of the tires, to drop or raise the track bar, how finally they got the car wicked fast, or failed.

I'm pregnant, a woman's voice had said.

Oh, I said.

It's his, and I—but she didn't finish and I didn't know how to help her.

We don't have any money, I warned, but her silence said that wasn't it either. How do you know it's him? I stalled for time.

I'd just gotten out when I met him, she began. I was too sad, you see, they said a person shouldn't be that sad, so they gave me a place to stay while I cheered up. I was doing a lot better so I went to that bar by the racetrack. It's where my brother always goes. He introduced us, my brother did. Now he's so mad. I'm sorry.

I knew the bar, knew he drank there although not a lot, not at that time. Didn't he tell you he was married? I asked. And I knew every word she was saying was true. Absolutely. Without a doubt. I'll have him call you, I told her. He's in North Carolina, but I'll have him call you, I promise.

I usually keep my promises. I'm the kind of person who can't say a thing unless it's true or I mean it to be true. At least I try. So I promised myself I'd get even that night, get even for his two unwanted, unplanned children. I did what I could. It took me a few tries, but before long, there was Verne with the bad teeth meeting me after work at the knickknack store, driving me out to the country to park in the dark Nebraska fields where we would kiss and do it. I held my breath against the rotting smell when he put his tongue in my mouth or breathed through my mouth when he put his mouth other places. It wasn't hard to imagine my husband's hands and lips instead of Verne's. I'd taught both of them, after all.

More booms from trees a block away splitting and crashing to the pavement, bouncing up and settling back down, quickly coating with ice like dissolved light solidifying again. I can hold the phone, listen, and watch through my windows all at once. This is how it looks out there now: white and absurdly bent. Tree limbs at new, impossible angles, like badly broken bones, the way you know there's been an accident.

The morning I came home from spending all night with Verne, after leaving the baby at the neighbor's, expecting my husband to be away at the Wilkes Barre Speedway like he said, he was waiting for me. I don't know how it happened that I put my hand in my coat pocket with the keys as I came through the door and then the surprise of seeing him sitting there, made me jerk it out and with it my diaphragm in that stupid pink disk that dropped and rolled toward him while we both watched it, in terror. Then it did what it was supposed to, fell to its flat side at his feet.

It wasn't like he beat me, though I tell women that when they ask. He slapped my face and back and shoulders and arms and chest, maybe once or twice a fist, but really, it was shoving and spitting, not beating. I tried to break a four foot mirror over him, but he grabbed it. Then I ran out the door and stopped, panting and shaking on the sidewalk. Maybe I was waiting. It took a few minutes for him to catch up, but when he did I began to walk quickly away with him behind me, spitting on me, cursing me, trying to hang onto my coat.

This is the story I don't tell my daughter. You can see why. Better to leave him as he is, harmless except for the nights he brings her crying to her knees like this. I intend to help her, you understand, though now she suspects me too. I won't leave her as he has, vulnerable to these feelings, wanting to hurt, or to hurt someone.

Don't call me for a while, she says at 3:30 A.M., don't offer me anything.

Okay, I promise, relieved that I won't have to give her the truth.

I just wanted to ask if it was alright to stop now, she says. I wasn't going to talk to you but I couldn't not ask. Is it okay, then? Is it okay not to care about him anymore? Not to keep trying to be the good person, the good daughter? Is it alright, can I just stop now? Please? She keeps the sobs knotted in her voice and I can hear them like a fist ready to explode.

All night I listen to the trees cracking like lightning around the house and marching down the streets radiating from this room. When I go out for errands late the next morning, my telephone wires pool in the side yard under their clear protective coat, halves of trees block streets, and everywhere shattered ice looks like casings of mutant insects as the sun temporarily warms and loosens their hold. Then at 2:00, the temperature drops again, the sky thickens and grays, and the trees begin to wave ferociously over the cars. I make myself drive under them, though I am the only one foolish enough to do so. It begins to sprinkle again as if the weather were a kind of danger finally biting through the skin of the world. At the stoplight before my block, I see crows trying to ride the ice rimmed branches at the tops of hundred-foot elms in the wind, black on white. And remember that in the sky at dawn now, there is a comet as big and white as an albino basketball we will be able to see just before it crashes into us. But that's not the truth of what has ruptured our lives, is it?

Billy Kitchen

"You have a destructive nature," the card said. "One of these days you'll go to a party and the course of your life will be altered. Your past life may have been very unhappy." Billy Kitchen always got warnings like this in fortune cookies and horoscopes. Now this card. He glanced up at the antique machine with the dusty puppet head of an old woman bearing a long hooked nose, warts, and glittery painted eyes that looked at him through a grimy film. "Grandmother's Prophesies," the sign said. He thought about putting another quarter in the slot, but decided to go with what he'd learned. His "luck numbers" were 514, 16, 17, 18, printed on the bottom of the lavender card. At the top was a pissed off cartoon man breaking a chair with his foot while he swung a yowling black cat around by the tail. Well, Billy hadn't swung the cat around, he'd picked it up and thrown it against the wall, followed by the pocket calculator which had just told him what he didn't want to hear late last night.

Billy turned the card over. Birdeene's birthday was in July, she was a Leo and her flower was larkspur, whatever the heck that was, and her birthstone was ruby, something he'd definitely have to save up for. Why couldn't she have been born an Aquarius with carnations and garnets, both recognizable and affordable? Or Capricorn with holly and turquoise so he could go right now over to the Southwestern stall and find her a ring? He craned his head to see if she was anywhere around, then spotted her over at the stuffed chicken booth. At least that's what he called it. When he asked the man where he got all those baby animals stuffed and standing or squatting in natural settings on little varnished boards, the man said they all died of natural causes. The chicks were at their appealing yellow fuzzy stage, as were the baby rabbits and squirrels. "Yeah right, carbon monoxide," Billy had muttered and pushed his way through the people crowding up to buy.

He just hoped Birdeene had enough sense not to bring home one of those stuffed babies. "Enough is enough," he'd told her last night after the cat and calculator hit the wall in one-two punches. But she wasn't the one who spent the money, he hadn't had to remind himself of that. Well, what difference did it make, he argued with himself. One way or the other, the money was gone. Sooner or later, he was going to have to go over and ask Merle Schemerhorn for a job at the Glory to God garage. Merle knew what he could do on an engine and had been reminding him of the job offer every Sunday for the past three months. At first, Billy had laughed with Birdeene about the idea, now it didn't seem so damn funny. Merle had more business than he could handle laying hands on cars to fix them and healing people's souls when they came to pay. But Billy had been raised Catholic and wasn't sure about this other stuff. He didn't like personal religion.

Four years ago when the priest at Holy Spirit in Saint Paul, Minnesota had said his name as he placed the wafer on his tongue, Billy had started going to other churches he didn't even belong to. "I'm the phantom communion taker," he told Birdeene when they met. "I bolt in and out. I don't know why Father Ignatius had to say, 'the Body of Christ, Billy,'" he complained. When they first moved to this small Iowa town, there was only one Catholic church so he couldn't go at all. Then Birdeene had taken him to her Pentecostal church and he'd met Merle and his family.

That was a year and a half ago when he was still drag racing his '73 Barracuda with the 470-cubic-inch Hemi engine. With two-stage nitrous injection, he could run an 8.91, over 150 MPH, but not at Bristol, Tennessee for the Mopar Southern Nationals because of the altitude. He'd worked his butt off, staying up most of the night trying to figure how to get more oxygen into the engine, but he'd been beaten in the first run by a '65 Coronet. The loss gave him time to pick up a Webster cylinder head that'd been nicely machined at the swap meet. And he'd been able to sell three of the early Chrysler model valve covers he'd toted around since last spring. He still wondered about not selling the car when he had the chance. Guy offered him $100,000 and he'd turned it down. Then he'd had the wreck on the line at Davenport. They'd taken a graft off his hip for his leg, and the collarbone had healed alright. He was covered by Birdeene's health insurance, but the car was totaled without insurance. It burned up after he pulled himself free. The Mickey Thompson slicks melted into smoldering black puddles on the grass by the time they got the fire under control. He hadn't let the ambulance take him away until he'd seen his car that one last time.

He was fine now. Not more than a twinge when the weather turned, and every farmer around here could tell you the same story. But he missed his car. Sometimes when he'd had a couple of beers, Billy told Birdeene how sorry he was that he hadn't sold the car at Bristol so it'd still be around. Other times he told her he didn't see how he could've sold the car and missed out on those last runs of the summer when he'd won two meets back to back.

Her father, Sumpter Yung, who farmed outside of town, had offered him work repairing machinery as soon as Billy could walk around on his air cast. He'd rebuilt one tractor engine from the ground up, got the other running smooth as butter, then fixed the combine and hayer and harrow. Sumpter had liked the work pretty well and sent Billy inside the house to work on the refrigerator.

After that it was the well pump and the Dodge Ram pickup which he almost had to rebuild, but for two months now, there'd been no new work and Billy was beginning to get worried. They lived okay off what Birdeene made doing books at the grain elevator and feed store, but it wasn't right. He couldn't spend her money and he was down to nothing now. Every penny gone with the calculator and the cat who'd picked itself up and burst through the old screening on the kitchen door, disappearing into the night. Despite being raised on a farm, Birdeene was very sentimental about animals so the cat going airborne had been between them since that fateful moment twelve hours ago. Billy glanced at her thick, sturdy back, square as a cereal box, considering whether the stuffed baby chicken was her idea of revenge. Should have gotten a kitten, but there'd been no puppies or kittens. Probably too close to home. People didn't care as much if a baby bird died.

The Counting Crows music from the giant caterpillar ride clashed with the loud Rolling Stones music from the roller coaster and the loudspeaker from the freak show. Billy looked toward the game booths where tattooed men leaned out trying to catch the attention of the passersby, cawing and whistling like greasy birds in their cages of balloons, floating ducks, basketball hoops, and thick, dingy metal milk bottles. Maybe he could win her something and get out from under all this bad luck.

Last night sitting in the backyard at the Yung farm after supper, Birdeene and her stepmother doing dishes while he and Sumpter watched Novelle, the youngest boy, gun the pickup engine a couple of times, then spin the tires in the gravel and roar fishtailing down the drive. Novelle was always trying to impress Billy with his driving skills, and Billy had to grin. The Hemi engine had been half-melted by the heat of the fire. It was sitting in some scrapyard now. There were just times you gave up, he told himself when he pictured the engine.

"I'm thinking about getting me a Normande cow," Sumpter had said after a while. When they sat down, the last rose had mounted the sky, dissolved against the blue-black and spilled down across the yard, then pulled back so completely a few minutes later they were sitting in the dark. The wind stirred the sycamores and lifted Billy's hair. "Good mothers, Normandes, real nice to work around. Have these dark udders won't get sunburned like your other cows. Dark markings around the eyes decrease chances of pink eye and cancer eye. Produces 9,240 pounds of milk a year. Think I might just try it. Upgrade the herd some."

The breeze felt cool and damp, as if it were blowing from somewhere rainy. Billy looked up at the dark, starless sky. "Rain coming." He never knew what to make of Sumpter's farm talk, so he stuck pretty much to weather. If Birdeene were out here, she could help. He knew they were coming to something. Sumpter had asked him out there for a reason.

"You know what women want, son?" Sumpter asked, his voice seeming to spring out of the dark at him.

He shook his head with the sudden despair of realization.

"They want you to read their minds, Billy."

He waited for Sumpter to go on, but the wind picked up and flapped the yard gate a couple of times. Billy got up and walked over to latch it. On the hill past the cow barn, he could see the lights of the neighbors blinking in the trees of the windbreak like ships on rough waters.

"Women think they can read minds, son. And we men know we can't even read lips," Sumpter said as soon as Billy sat down in the canvas folding chair that slung his butt scraping along the grass beneath him.

"Sounds right." He always agreed with Birdeene's father.

"So you have to ask yourself, son, what does she want? What is she trying to ask for that I should but can't read in her mind?" Sumpter loaded a cigarette in his mouth and snapped it alive with a wooden kitchen match. Drawing, he let out the smoke in a long sigh.

That was when Billy knew he was getting married to Birdeene. It was his job to buy the ring, ask her, convince her it was the right thing, and then actually go through with it. Trouble was, he was broke and he couldn't let her pay for her own ring. He'd been around long enough to see how that kind of bargain brought a person to grief sooner or later down the line. He thought of the 'Cuda again. Losing her was an awful lot like losing a loved one. Birdeene had been the first to realize that. For the first few months, she'd been the one pushing him to see about another car, bringing home the free *Auto Shopper* from the Quik Stop, but she'd stopped when she saw how he let them pile up on the table beside their bed.

Then he found the pamphlet on grief from Sons Funeral Home under the weekly county newspaper on the kitchen counter and had secretly read it himself. There were quotations that began and ended each chapter, most of them uplifting in a relentless way, but he had found one he copied and carried in his wallet now: "A man's worth of ashes is an easily handled jar." In his mind he added, "but not a car's," every time he glanced at the paper. Losing a car was a lot like losing a horse, it was too big to get rid of easily. Mostly he couldn't stand the idea of the car scrapped out and the engine stranded like a giant, half-melted ice cube. The engine alone had cost him two years of scraping and saving, working two jobs and trading every single thing he owned except his tools and trophies. But it wasn't the money, he realized as he read about the ten stages of grief. It wasn't the trophies and ribbons either, though he'd put them away in a box he'd shoved up into the attic crawlspace as soon as he was able to negotiate the pull-down ladder.

Billy turned away from the midway rides and game booths. Birdeene was still in line for the stuffed baby chicken, her dollars sticking out between her fingers while she looked anxiously around her. Probably for him, he decided and ducked into a group of people pushing toward the line of merchandise stands backing the grandstand for the drag strip and racecourse behind the dirt bank and tall wooden fence.

"Billy Kitchen!" Merle Schemerhorn's voice reached its long arm over the heads of people making him turn back. The wide bearded face with the pale gray eyes the color of the cat he'd punished for being nothing but alive at the wrong moment floated toward him even though he tried to back away.

When they shook hands, Merle put his other hand over Billy's and trapped him so they were standing in the middle of the fair holding hands. Billy glanced over Merle's shoulder to see if anyone was noticing, but Merle kept his wide smile and cat-gray eyes right on him. Billy tried to push away the tide of goodwill rolling off the other man like sweat.

"So Birdeene says you're finally coming to work." Merle squeezed his hand one more time and let go. When Billy took a step back, Merle put a hand on his shoulder. "We need you, boy. Mrs. Wilborn up and died and left the ministry her son's car, a '70 Dodge Challenger the boy bought just before he went to Viet Nam. His mother was a widow and that boy was her only living relative. Couldn't bear to sell the car, you see." Merle's fingers kneaded his shoulder in an almost painful way. "It's an awful nice car, Billy, 5,000 miles on it. Figured you could see about cleaning the engine up, do what's needed to get it running good after all those years of sitting in her shed."

Billy twisted away, and couldn't stop himself from rubbing his shoulder. "I don't know, Merle—"

"Sure, we'll hold you up to the Lord and get you running good as new too." His face turned serious. "There are lots of opportunities to minister, Billy, you have to do whatever the Lord gives you a chance to do."

"I—"

"Hey, Tug—" Merle stuck out a hand and neatly sidestepped Billy's clouded expression.

After that Billy let himself drift with the crowd of people licking ice cream and snow cones, chewing french fries and corn dogs as they shuffled past displays for night driving glasses, vibrating foot massagers, advanced design floor mops, car wax, sonic jewelry cleaning machines, and computer personality tests. He didn't mean to pause at the Christian sales table with the special magnifying glasses embossed with gold crosses on the clear plastic handles, plaster Jesus heads, and rosary beads, but the people carrying him along had gradually dispersed to the booths and goods along the way until he was single again, landing the way a boat does, nudging the wooden table. Although his quick survey revealed nothing useful to him, the woman sitting on a folding chair behind the table began to lift tiredly from her seat. Then his eye caught on the Gravestone Decoration Holder on the pegboard behind her. She lifted it off the hook and held it out to him until he took it. "Flexible steel bends to fit the thickness of stone or easily pushes into the ground for a stand-up display like this." She took it out of his hands and stood it on the counter for him. "This plastic strip adjusts to hold different size decorations. See?" She wiggled it at him. "Can use it year-round too." She placed it carefully in his hands again. He sure didn't want this. "Fair special: $3.99." He could see that was the regular price on the tag. "Two for seven dollars. Most folks need more than one." He tried to hand it back, but she kept her hands below the countertop and he felt awkward about just laying it on the sad eyes of the Jesus paper napkins wrapped in brittle old cellophane.

"Okay, well—I'll think about it." He eased the metal holder down without looking at her or the booth again and slipped away. It made him feel strange, all this religion. That was the thing about a small town, everyone inspecting the inside of your shirt collar, the dirt on your soul. He did not want to be this personal with God. He didn't question himself about these things, it was like asking yourself if you were really going to win a race, you had to act like you would. You had to do the best you could on the car, get a good roll, quick off the line, that's what it was all about. Now where in the hell was he going to get a ring for Birdeene?

He stood on his tiptoes and scanned the crowd and fair booths. He saw Birdeene coming toward him with a brown paper bag cradled against her chest like a baby, he saw Merle Schemerhorn with his arm around the shoulders of Novelle, Birdeene's youngest brother whose bent head revealed the shaved white line of his new haircut, he thought he saw Sumpter leaning against the white board fence of the livestock judging ring filled with dark red and white-spotted cattle, each one bespectacled with dark patches around the eyes, but he didn't see himself. When it was all said and done, it came to Billy, there was something mercenary about his grief, and while he milked it for everything he could get, he always seemed to be broke.

Caution

Many and deep are the wounds of the living, my mother used to warn me those last days of waiting in her high, four-poster bed. On this early Pennsylvania Christmas morning, I have to ask how Magda could not want the bells you can hear clear across dawn with the sky already light from snow. I mean, it is not the first time I have sat thus at my little kitchen window waiting for the bright surprised pink. Nor the birds who rise up from the trees with a cry as if startled awake again at the moment, the uttermost moment they had given in to darkness. In this, his dusty disguise, a hawk lands in the icy snow patch where I throw out bread of a morning and waits motionless for the small birds to come feed. He turns his head in slow motion, his beak a curve of disaster, and watches the brush, the bread, the brush, while overhead on the limb of the big twisted apple tree a crow looks down, waiting with a curious eye, craning its neck to see me and the hawk both.

My only interference is getting up for more tea, and my motion sends the scene scurrying. Well, it is true that I held my place carefully in the days Magda was racing. I daren't move a wink. It was such magic the music of engines and tires, the audible sight catching and weaving us into its bright roaring ribbon around and around the track. High on the banks, low in the turns. My heart with every revolution, turning older and older.

It's not often you get to see your life making progress. Magda was named for my mother, and with half the wisdom, she lifted herself off the porch into her first car at the age of twelve. There was no stopping her then. Albert said you cannot stop will like that. He'd had it as a boy, such a look in that body, and I had let it be. Ours is not the life you see paper-clipped to the bottom of the page. There has been small attention paid to the after, after it's over. Albert gave her all his wildness and I gave what I could. Judgment, not the kind you earn, but the kind you arrive with. Magda, knowing how to run through those gears without a glance. Some drivers do it by sound, they brag, but she could feel the car pulling to the pitch past its own restraint, then, then, like the tip of a sharp needle, she was that precise. Judgment. The tires as they begin to go away, this is how she described it.

It was not the usual homecoming. She was battered, bruises across her thighs and across her stomach and chest and back like she'd been on a ladder run over lightly by a train. She spent hours in the bathroom off the kitchen, soaking in the old claw foot tub. It was on one of those occasions that she began to tell me how she could feel the car, the metal itself like a high and gorgeous song through the helmet and earplugs and head protecting gear.

It's our bodies they forget to cover, our bodies that think out there. Sometimes, Mama, sometimes there are just too many voices the car makes and I have to remember to pay attention.

I was sitting behind her on the pressed-back chair from my grandmother's set, each of us girls got one when they took her out of the house at the bottom of that dead end road to the quarry. I always wanted to live there. I remembered that, looking out the window facing the back hills which rose up behind us, blocking the light until well into morning and taking it away early each night. The horses were eating and arguing with the flies. The dog had something worrying it, trotting back and forth on this side of the creek that cut the pasture into a V. Albert was up in the high field on the tractor cultivating the corn. There was a distant white blue sky that said this had nothing to do with it. But the pine trees leaned down the hill at us, and if I looked hard enough, I could hear them whispering. The water in the creek got sluggish as syrup in August, so tired it could barely push itself choking over the rocks. And just outside the screen, mud daubers were making another stab at building onto the house. I still like to watch their inclinations. The way they walk up the screen, feeling for the spaces in the grid of wire squares. It is a familiar gesture. And sometimes I didn't listen as closely to Magda as I should have. Sometimes I watched instead.

But the tires, when they start to go away the track gets so slick. And during pit stops, they have to clean the pieces of rubber off the windshield and especially the grill to keep the engine from overheating.

No, I wanted to say, when they're worn, tires are leaking and peeling, scalding and shredding, those are my words for it. You have to be able to describe the terrain to yourself, otherwise the images mound up like discarded tires and something comes along and sets fire to your whole life, and you've seen the way those tires molder black and moody for days and weeks.

Magda used her toes to let more hot water into the tub, and I admired how well they'd healed, not crooked at all after that one time. She was in midgets on dirt tracks when that happened. It prepared me for the worst, you could say, but you wouldn't be right. Maybe it is the difficulty of seeing the thing you built, molded and made, torn down piece by piece, each fracture and cut another insult. I was angry seeing those toes because the black ridges on the nails never went away. She used to laugh and offer to paint them red to please me, but that was not what I meant. Maybe she understood all along and was only trying to make it easier. Albert up in the high field on his tractor. That worry. And Magda barred with bruises in the lukewarm water flecked with leaves of lavender and mint, my mother's recipe from her mother.

The tires, Mama. They have this whiny hum like an angry bee and a familiar vibration that comes up your legs and settles around your waist. You can feel it in your wrists and all the way up to your elbows.

Magda keeps her eyes closed as she tells me this. Her hair is floating brown around her shoulders. She has my mother's coloring, not mine. Her skin doesn't yellow up after the summer sun, or go blue-white by Christmas. It has something else in it. Albert maybe. I can see the little tufts of hair under her arms, collecting bubbles and bits of crushed leaves. She doesn't do the "girly thing" now. What did I expect? Maybe it is my mystery that I never guessed. Never imagined her beyond each day, never saw her living a such-and-such life.

When they're cold, the tires are hard, blocky. It hurts my body, like jumping out of the hay loft on cold feet. Then they soften and give as the heat comes up in them and suddenly we're racing. Like a horse taking the bit. There are just so many laps the tires are good for though, then they start to go away again, their voices changing, wobbling, gusty and—I don't know, but they're running away from me, scattering, and I have to chase them down before we wash up the track into the wall.

Magda. I hear the chug chug of the tractor echoing briefly out of the hills and then it's gone again. The horses don't lift their heads. The dog has settled to chewing something, a rabbit maybe, tearing at it, stretching the fur of it held between his front paws, pulling and stretching until I am so maddened by the sight I almost get up and go down there.

You should see how blue the sky can be. On a winter morning like this, it radiates. So blue, blue. How could she not have waited for this?

I never said no. Mothers are all alike.

Albert and I weren't there that day. Never intended to be there. Too far to go, we said. That wasn't the one we planned on attending. We were watching the race on television.

Magda was not a large girl, nor a particularly slender or graceful one either. I could see that well enough in the body that half floated before me that afternoon. Her thick calves and ankles, sturdy thighs, and straight hips and waist.

My mother, a southern lady married badly to a Pennsylvania miner, would have made her learn to dance to improve that clumsy bumping into chairs she did. But I wanted—what? I can't even say. I wanted to let her grow by herself. I was curious. I don't know how she discovered what made her graceful at last. Maybe it was the horses and then they weren't enough either. I can't say. But she was a girl who needed to clothe herself more. She was born too naked maybe. I can say that. Watching her in the tub that day, I came to understand how the racecar was a shell, how it added what she was born without. We all spend our days building and rebuilding, mudding up the mound we will crawl into. It seems human to need to do so, human and more.

She picked up the plastic cup and spilled water over her chest and shoulders while she talked. Her breasts, what a thing, to look on a daughter's breasts, but Magda had lost her modesty by then. Her work was too physical for that kind of luxury. So I let myself look, over and over, quick and then long, so I would remember every single thing. As if I must have already known, as if I could feel our lives running into trouble on the curves ahead. Her breasts were small and efficient, with tiny nipple buds I looked at as if they were the first fatality. I felt it wrong what I thought that afternoon—that she'd never have children with breasts like those. A mother can be so damning. Can damn herself as well. Because I wanted to throw the towel I was holding on my lap into the tub and say, cover yourself, and save us all, but of course I didn't.

You keep hoping for a yellow flag, a caution, not that you want anyone to get hurt, of course, but you need to change the tires. You always need to change the tires. There's only so many laps, then they go away and you try to hold the car together for a few more laps so that maybe, you're praying, maybe there's a yellow and you can pit without losing too much time or position. Unless everyone has to pit under green. But you know this, Mama. You've watched enough races. I just thought I could get another lap or two out of the tires, but they fooled me. I was listening and feeling them, but they got crazy all of a sudden out of turn two, and I thought, no, I've run over something, but I think the right front was going flat by then and that was the problem. I gave 'em the yellow that afternoon.

She is telling me the tire story for the first time, but by the end of the visit a week later, I will have heard it five more times. She moves the details a little each telling. She is fingering the wound, putting pressure on it to see where the greatest hurt lives. I should tell her she doesn't need to do this. Any of it. I try to picture the murmuring motion that lives in her, see it as that all-day train ride down to see my sister in Charlottesville. How my body keeps traveling the bump bumping tracks even when I'm in bed that night. My daughter is haunted. Listening to the motion her cells have memorized. She speaks from its prison, her voice traveling a great distance through the hot damp twilight of the bathroom to where I am sitting. But the mutterings outside the window keep growing louder, demanding my attention. So it is that I thrust her from me, this battered body, this wound I cannot bear.

Maybe she was waiting for me to say don't go back. You don't have to go back there. Maybe it was the water cooling for the final time that made her sigh and rise naked and maybe not even born yet, climb one foot at a time out onto the white-and-blue rag rug and pat her skin with the towel I silently handed her. A mother's hand, I couldn't touch her. Would not reach even a fingertip to the eggplant-colored bruise across the back of her shoulders. Got up and left the room before she could ask me to cover her back with the turquoise menthol heat cream. Pretended not to hear her calling for help.

Kept walking to the far room where I sat at the sewing machine once more, but couldn't get a straight seam in the green dress I was making her. Got up and walked outdoors, ignoring her call again. Walked to the kitchen garden and saw everything bursting ripe and yellow and dry. A flock of red-wing blackbirds swept across my path so close their wings pushed my breath back, and I flung a hand out to stop them but they were too quickly gone. I followed the path through the pasture, across the creek, and up the hill toward Albert and the sound of his tractor I was just beginning to pick up. And I didn't once look back at the porch with the rust-stained screens where her puzzled face waited that last time.

Mystery of Numbers

Tom was having that emergency recall of the conscience he always got Christmas Eve, but the car was due at
the track two days from now for testing, and there wasn't a damn
thing he could do about it. He tried to fit the headers back on
the engine, still not right. He sighed and rubbed his face on his
sleeve. Sometimes he wondered if he'd ever get the hang of it
here. His last job, several years ago now, had been at Larold
Martin's Chix-N-Stuff which everyone thought was a topless
place until they got inside and saw the sign—Chicken Fingers!
The Real Choice!—and smelled the deep fryers which were what
eventually got them closed because Quinta, Larold's sister and
general manager, refused to change the grease more than once a
month and first that nice black couple from Des Moines and
then Larold's baby girl and then the town alderman all got sick.
Not close-to-death sick, but pretty darn sick considering all
they were trying to do was fries and fingers and a Coca-Cola,
which should be by God safe in this day and age. That's what
Larold told them as he fired the lot, Tom ducking through the
door under Speed Maxwell's crane coming to take down the sign
and hoist up another for Larold's new place called Come N Git It!
All in all, he guessed this job working for his dad's garage was a
heck of a lot steadier, even if the hours were out-of-this-world
long.

Tom still wouldn't go to Larold's again, not even if it was the only place open on a Sunday night when he was done working sixteen hours straight with only vending-machine candy bars and soda pop till his stomach was shaking hands with his backbone. Some nights he could feel the burning cramp all the way up his shoulders, as he tried to force stale bread with the cold sleeve of the refrigerator on it down his throat between gulps of water before he climbed tired as death into bed next to Marie who was, all in all, a good woman, if a bit vengeful. She didn't mind him putting his cold butt up next to her stomach and always clamped that one leg over his like now she had him she wasn't going to let him go, even though his feet were two icy bricks.

He was the one needed warming in bed, and she was the one to do it. Marie was a big woman, tall and thick-boned as an axe handle, his daddy Red had said when Tom showed up at the garage with her. Red Yearly'd looked eye to eye with Marie and said something—it was lost now with a lot of other useless items—but what Marie had said always stuck in Tom's mind of a morning when he combed his hair carefully forward and then back, looking for the telltale pink between the heavy brown waves. "Bald can take you someplace," she'd replied and Red smiled, lifting the side of his lip so those pick-sharp canines showed.

Red thought he looked like Elvis when he did that, but Tom thought his daddy really looked more like Scout, their skinny brown bird dog. Although he was tied by a long rope attaching him most days and nights of his life to the cottonwood out front of the garage, the dog never bothered trying to chew his way loose. It was the same tree with the block and tackle suspended overhead from the thickest limb ready to noose an engine up and out of a car. Tom figured maybe the dog had watched that enough times to imagine its brown useless body going up too because Scout was the least trouble a dog could be in the world and in the emergency recall of his conscience this Christmas Eve, Tom could see how that was a wrong thing. That dog living its quiet, terrified life under the chain of its demise. He should at least bark.

Tom argued the dog's case with Red this morning, but his father was incapable of seeing how the humped back and curled head were the signs of something deeper than a bad gene pool. He'd gotten Scout from a pig farmer in trade for the salvage carburetor on an '86 Olds Ciera whose black finish was sanded salt-gray before the farmer got the car from his cousin in trade for Scout's mother and two pigs, Scout's mother being one of the best bird dogs this side of the Mississippi, according to everyone in the county. No reason that pig farmer should have a dog that nice, Red commented as the Olds drove off and left the puppy cowering flat at their feet.

But truth be told, Scout was afraid of loud noises from the git-go, hated so when his feet got even a hint of damp that he learned to climb trees just to stay out of the weather. The rope was long enough to let him up into the crotch of the cottonwood where he'd wait out just about any sort of change, and the dog had long ago learned not to tangle himself going up and down. "Maybe he should be a coon dog," Red remarked about once a week when he noticed the milk-brown eyes in the tree staring down at them as Tom came to work of a morning. "I got him that perfectly good doghouse too," Red would gesture toward the fifty-gallon drum on its side, streaked with rust and the tiny dents from that hail-storm last summer which had done a job on one of the racecars too. Fred Creed had shown up with all the bad luck of that sum-mer right after the storm let up and had one of his royal fits. "As in fit to be tied, and about to be fired," Red called it.

Creed's kid Bobby was trying to be a race driver and Creed's Ford Lincoln Mercury dealership was one of his sponsors, along with his vacuum cleaner repair business which was a front for God knew what, but Tom figured there couldn't be that many bum vacuums in the entire county or nobody would have a clean house. "It's nothing." Red would pat his son on the back when he saw him getting those suspicions on his face in little lines around his mouth and between his eyes. "Tom, you worry about all the wrong things," his father would explain and nod toward the engine they were rebuilding. "Now mill that deck so we can squeeze another mile or two out of this thing. I think I figured this thing with the cylinder heads we can get away with."

It was Red's little innovations kept them in the racing engine business while Tom did the everyday car repair work. "Father and son," Red would announce every year when they posed arm in arm for their Christmas card with the shop as the backdrop, a racecar gleaming beside them and the dog peering out of the tree at them like a demented squirrel. They always looked exactly like father and son, Tom noted as soon as the cards arrived from the print shop. Red, the tall father, Marie's size really, and Tom, the short, compact son. It wasn't easy being a small man, but he didn't discuss it. Marie found him satisfactory in that way that women find a man more or less, but some days he felt like that dog, like maybe he needed to climb a tree to get a better view of things, because right now he felt like a stump in the woods.

Christmas Eve, even the Wal-Mart closed at six, Larold's at eight. Bobby wanted a car could run both the high side and the white line on the bottom of the track. Red had picked up the magnesium housing for the transmission shipped in from Richmond yesterday, same as Winston Cup cars used, and said they could find the horsepower. "Maybe the spring rate's wrong." Tom had tried to convince Red of something hours ago so they could go home and have a decent Christmas Eve, but Red had reminded him they were engine men—their first job was engine, not chassis. "Bobby's living in a fantasy world," Tom had muttered, "so's the old man. Kid couldn't drive a mail truck let alone a racecar."

"Last race the power-steering belt came off and took the oil belt," Red reminded him and went to the workbench where he sat for hours writing numbers and making little drawings on graph paper while Tom started grinding the head deck. Late summer when Dale Earnhardt had driven into the wall at the start of the Mountain Dew Southern 500, they said he experienced "a transient alteration of his consciousness." Tom was thinking he needed one of those, but hoped it wouldn't take a smack in the wall to do it. When he called her at eight to say he was going to be a little bit longer before he'd be home to play Santa Claus, Marie had hissed, "I want a man in an Elvis suit," and slammed down the phone.

"Need to adjust that compression ratio and keep some fuel mileage," Red announced after the phone call. "I'm going out for a bit. Want anything? I'll think better with some fresh coffee." Red had wet what remained of his hair and combed it flat against the back of his skull. "Sex on the hoof," Marie had called him.

It wasn't long after Marie showed up, Red quit trying to fool anybody about his hair. Now she was cutting it once a month along with Tom's, her long white fingers pulling the thin strands away from the scalp, holding them there for a moment, the scissors poised, then the snip in a clean line that left Tom a little breathless. Sometimes lately, he didn't know why it bothered him to see her standing behind the chair with her hands resting on his father's shoulders for that brief time while the old man looked at himself in the mirror. Marie changed when she cut hair. Grew distance like grass, a whole yard-full he couldn't quite get across, like in a dream where your legs wouldn't stand up for themselves, or like Red when he was at his graphs and numbers. There wasn't anything Tom did he couldn't feel or think to himself, here I am, here I am.

Every time that damn Bobby Creed blew the engine from running the RPMs too high too long, Tom took it personally. While his heart thumped and the first stink of sweat rose off the son trying to control his anger, Red would be walking around the engine block tapping his short fingers with the thick orange hairs against his wide grizzled jaw. While Red started making notes with the yellow pencil corrugated with teeth marks up and down the shaft, Tom had to be careful not to pick up a sledgehammer and smash the engine. Marie was like Red. Tom was the one weeping and confused when he was tired from twenty hours and no food, while Marie could always say what she wanted. And she had.

Tom looked over at Red with his head resting in his arms, snoring loudly now. He tightened the last bolt and straightened his back which hurt like a bastard from the hours of concentrated leaning over the motor. There was always something pure about the engine at this moment. He pulled the rag out of his back pocket and wiped a smudge from the valve cover. Maybe this would be the one, an engine the kid couldn't hurt, one that would take him sailing around the track as fast and as safe as his heart desired. See, he rubbed at another spot until he realized it was a shadow cast by the angle of light from the overhead fluorescents, it was the same as a new car or new house or even a new job or wife when he finished an engine. All promise, all hopefulness. He felt what he thought a person must feel for their child when he looked at the engine, though he knew other people like Marie only saw a chunk of metal. He swiped at it again and was going to stick the rag in his pocket when Red snorkeled a little and moved his hand, tipping over the Styrofoam cup and spilling the last drops of coffee on the papers.

Without disturbing his father, Tom picked up the cup and dabbed at the spill with his rag until only a few dark bits of grounds remained. He thought about waking Red or pulling the damp papers away from the arm anchoring them to the bench, but did neither. Although the coffee had blurred them somewhat, the fractions and ratios seemed at first to move in a kind of church processional across the pages, then they seemed to clump and fuse, collect and gather, before releasing as random as water down the page. Tom carefully pulled the papers from under Red's arms without waking him and held them more directly under the light. In some weird dance they partnered with sketches of cylinders and carburetors, pistons and sparkplugs, the engine taken to pieces, shaved by fractions until they found the exact degree where the metal could be thinnest and most whole, reconfigured to produce and sustain the most horsepower.

"It's Christmas," he muttered half loud enough for Red to maybe hear. The snoring paused, took a deep honk, then proceeded in a new key. Tom had this urge to touch his father's shoulder, to run his hand along the orange-white hairs of his arm, to see if he could feel the thousands of freckles stranded on the yellow-pink skin like tiny planets in a reverse sky. Replacing the papers on the bench, he held his hand over his father's, wanting to slide fingers in between fingers, while his shadow hovered larger in blunt definition, cuffing veins and pores with darkness. They weren't the same hands, father to son, Tom recognized. He had his mother's hands, her coloring and size. There was almost nothing of his father stamped on him except the shape of his head and his eyes maybe, the brown eyes that in his father seemed to pick up the orange-red glow of his skin and hair, while in Tom they remained the truer brown of brown. That's how he thought of it. Marie had said it so it must be true.

For almost the first time, looking at the tired slump of his father's back, Tom wondered about Red living alone out back in the trailer he'd bought after his wife died. Before that, it was Tom living in the basement of the house half a mile down the road from the garage with his parents thumping around upstairs while he worked at one job or another and finally Larold's. When his mother died of cancer, the two men seemed to run from the place, which was now rented to a young couple from the Teaching Corps who helped out at the rural school fifteen miles away. Although they had an old Chevy, they usually rode their bikes back and forth to work when it wasn't raining or snowing, with so many books stuck in the saddlebag baskets behind, Tom could see the muscles in the woman's calves straining with the load up the hill from the house. Once they'd had trouble starting their car, and Tom had driven them to work in the rain and come back and changed the plugs and oil, adjusted the timing, and cleaned things up in general. He knew the Chevy Cavalier never liked to work in the rain because Powell had owned it until he donated it to the County Vo Tech for rehabilitation. Now Tom got to keep working on it every time the season changed. He hadn't the heart to stay in the house after his mother died or to tell that young couple the truth about their car either.

He met Marie the day after the funeral when he and Red went out to Axel's to have a couple of mournful drinks and he moved in with her the next night. Red had gone off on his own some-where with Mrs. Rankin, the widow from Oskaloosa who came to visit her sister Meryl on weekends so she could raise a little hell away from her neighbors. It had only seemed fitting for the two of them to find solace in their mutual grief, Marie had remarked, as she emptied her screwdriver, sucked the ice, and held up the glass for another. She was just back from beauty college in Des Moines and opening her own place in the basement of the walk-out her dad had left her when he died a year before. Marie found a place for Tom in her life about 1 A.M. that night when the lights came up and they staggered out the door together. He was even better-looking in the daylight, she announced the next morning and got up to cook him eggs over-easy and fresh thick country bacon from her uncle's pig farm. It was her uncle who had owned Scout's mother and left the dog with them a few weeks later. The whole family had been worried to death about Marie until Tom came along, he said.

Nobody mentioned marriage, but it happened right along with everything else. Within a year of burying his mother and meet-ing Marie in the bar, Tom walked down the aisle of the Christ Community Church and said he did to her I do and had a big meal and a car trip to Chicago for the weekend. He hadn't thought directly about his father living in the trailer for four years until now. Hadn't worried. Red was in better physical shape than Tom most days, and Marie always mentioned how good he looked when she cut his hair, so there hadn't been the need for concern. His father showed up clean and ready to work every morning, commenting only on Scout or the engines they worked on, while the days and months flooded by, notable only for the need to open or close the big front garage doors and turn on or off fans and heaters.

So now it was Christmas Eve, no, Tom corrected himself, early Christmas Day. The twenty-fifth. Should he wake Red and take him back to the trailer, or leave him here to wake himself? He hadn't been inside his father's place in over a year, maybe two years now. They met in the garage or Red came to the house to eat a meal when Marie invited him or to get his hair cut. What was back there anymore? He hadn't ever remembered Red cooking when his mom was alive . . . did he cook now? All he knew about the man were the scrawls on the papers in front of him. Hell, he didn't even know if the widow from Oskaloosa was still coming down to see him on Saturday nights.

What did he know, what did he really know about anybody else? His wife wanted a man in an Elvis suit and the stores were closed. He'd gotten her a new dishwasher for Christmas and at 9 A.M., only a matter of hours from now, Floyd from Seiffert's Appliance was going to deliver it with a big smile and red paper bow. And Red, well, he'd gotten him a new toolchest from Sears, the big dresser size to replace the one Bobby had backed the car into last month. But that wasn't the same, was it? The same as what, Tom couldn't say, but he knew he was somehow in trouble here. Recently he was coming to see that maybe Marie was right when she said desire was an educational process. Since Marie showed up four years ago, his mind was irrigated by possibility. Like those numbers his father arranged and rearranged, something sang to him while he spun shreds of metal with the grinder or checked the cathode color of the spark plugs, something whispered and promised him more than memories, more than he could understand, something which Marie saw when he called a little while ago again to tell her he was coming home soon, only a matter of minutes, he promised, and she told him he was eternally and fatally optimistic.

The clock over the workbench said 2 A.M. He turned up the heat and draped a coat over Red's shoulders. His father, nested down in those numbers, was probably going to be stiff in the morning, but he'd make it to their house for Christmas dinner like always. There'd be the usual distraction as Marie gave Red extra nice cuts of meat and made sure his coffee was hot the way he liked it, but Tom would try to ignore that business like always.

Outside, the dog lay shivering on the frozen ground in front of the oil drum, his eyes watery with moonlight as Tom started past, then noticed that the rope was wrapped around the tree trunk so Scout was held to the ground for a change. "Here," he said, and unsnapped the dog's collar.

For a moment, the dog waited, then stood cautiously, stretching in front with his head up and teeth bared in a grin, then behind with his head down so far his neck bones crunched and he shook himself all over before he took a couple of prancing steps forward, collecting his body like a horse.

"Good boy," Tom said and clapped his hands, but the dog ignored him and trotted around the driveway and tree a couple of times, sniffing and peeing on any object over a foot high, until finally he went to the garage and stood whining at the door. While Tom watched, the dog got more anxious, wagging his tail, jittering on his feet, until he jumped up and barked with a surprising high, loud voice, letting his claws squeal all the way down the metal door. In a moment, the door opened, and a pale hand came out and motioned for the dog to come in, then the door closed. It didn't surprise Tom as much as it might have a few hours ago, seeing his father take that dog inside which he must have been doing all along judging from the little ritual. Then it dawned on him that they might have been waiting for Tom to leave all those nights he worked late on the motors. That Red wouldn't want his son to know how he'd taken to babying the dog. And the dog especially waiting out here in the cold must have hoped the son would go home to his young wife sooner than he frequently did.

Tom folded his arms, tucking his hands into his pits to keep them warm while he stood beside the tree watching the garage for any other sign of activity, but there was only the silence of a deep winter night, frost clinging to car windows and fuzzing the sheet metal walls and roof of the garage. He thought about his father in there working the numbers again, divining, imagining them into new relationships. Twenty-four, that's how old Tom was, four years with Marie, three years married, four years and change working at the garage here, ten years since he could drive, four since he could drink legally, 10/23 his birthday, 5/30 Marie's, 7/11 Red's. These were the only numbers he cared about—the rest belonged to his father or anyone else who wanted to claim them, like that lady out east who saw the winning lottery numbers in her sleep. He figured they were hung low like clouds for some people to grab, and high as stars for people like him.

He stood there watching the yellow-white light of the garage, his breath a slow stream as he felt his toes grow cold as if the frozen dirt gripped up at him. Occasionally something would sigh or creak with that high squeak of the very cold, but the stillness was absolute and pure, as if Tom himself had willed it so, and in this moment anything at all could come true, and all he could think of was that it be this, this very world at his feet, all around him, and then he hoped that somehow, when he finally crawled into bed tonight, he could think of a way to convince Marie that he was as much Elvis as she might want or need on Christmas Day.